We Run the Tides

ALSO BY VENDELA VIDA

The Diver's Clothes Lie Empty

The Lovers

*Confidence, or the Appearance of Confidence:
The Best of the Believer Music Interviews* (co-ed.)

The Believer Book of Writers Talking to Writers (ed.)

Let the Northern Lights Erase Your Name

And Now You Can Go

Girls on the Verge

We Run the Tides

A Novel

Vendela Vida

HARPER LARGE PRINT

An Imprint of **HarperCollins***Publishers*

WE RUN THE TIDES. Copyright © 2021 by Vendela Vida. All rights reserved. Printed in the United States of America. No part of this book may be used or reproduced in any manner whatsoever without written permission except in the case of brief quotations embodied in critical articles and reviews. For information, address HarperCollins Publishers, 195 Broadway, New York, NY 10007.

HarperCollins books may be purchased for educational, business, or sales promotional use. For information, please e-mail the Special Markets Department at SPsales@harpercollins.com.

FIRST HARPER LARGE PRINT EDITION

ISBN: 978-0-06-306313-6

Library of Congress Cataloging-in-Publication Data is available upon request.

21 22 23 24 25 LSC 10 9 8 7 6 5 4 3 2 1

*This book is dedicated to
my childhood friends and teachers,
who will immediately recognize
that this is a work of fiction.*

Why must a girl pay so dearly for her least escape from routine? Why could one never do a natural thing without having to screen it behind a structure of artifice?

—EDITH WHARTON, *THE HOUSE OF MIRTH*

1984–1985

1

We are thirteen, almost fourteen, and these streets of Sea Cliff are ours. We walk these streets to our school perched high over the Pacific and we run these streets to the beaches, which are cold, windswept, full of fishermen and freaks. We know these wide streets and how they slope, how they curve toward the shore, and we know their houses. We know the towering brick house where the magician Carter the Great lived; he had a theater inside and his dining-room table rose up through a trapdoor. We know that Paul Kantner from Jefferson Starship lived or maybe still does live in the house with the long swing that hangs above the ocean. We know that the swing was for China, the daughter he had with Grace Slick. China was born the same year we were, and whenever we pass the house we look for China on the swing. We know the imposing salmon-colored house that had a party at which masked robbers appeared; when a female guest wouldn't relinquish her ring, they cut off her finger. We know where our school tennis instructor lives (dark blue tudor decorated with cobwebs every Halloween), where the school's dean of admissions lives (white house with black gate)—both are women, both are wives. We know where the doctors and lawyers live, and where the multi-generation San Franciscans live, the kind of people whose family names are associated with mansions and hotels in other parts of the city. And most important, because we are thirteen and attend an all-girls' school, we know where the boys live.

We know where the tall boy with webbed feet lives. Sometimes we watch Bill Murray movies with him and his friends at his house on Sea View Terrace and marvel at the way the boys can recite all the lines the way we know every word of *The Outsiders*. We know where the boy lives who breaks my necklace one day by the beach—it's a silver chain my mother gave me and he pulls it violently and I run from him. We know where the boy lives who comes to my house the day I get a canopy bed and, mistaking it for a bunk bed, climbs up and breaks it. It's never properly fixed and from then on the four posts tilt west. We suspect this boy and his friends are responsible for writing in the wet cement outside our school, the Spragg School for Girls. "Spragg is for girls who like to bragg," the cement says. It's hard to tell if the words were traced with a finger or a stick, but the imprint is deep. Ha! we say. They don't even know how to spell "brag."

We know where the cute boy whose father is in the Army lives. He just moved to San Francisco and he wears short-sleeve plaid shirts that were the style in the Great Lakes town he came from. We know his father must have a position that's fairly high up because otherwise why wouldn't he live in the Presidio where most people in the Army live? We spend little time thinking about Army hierarchy because their haircuts are so sad. We know where the boy with one arm lives, though we don't know how he lost it. He often plays tennis at the park on 25th Avenue or badminton in the alleyway behind his house, which is the alleyway that leads to my house. Many of the blocks in Sea Cliff have alleyways so the cars can park in the garages in the back, so the cars don't interfere with the view of the ocean, of the Golden Gate Bridge. Everything in Sea Cliff is about the view of the bridge. It was one of the first neighborhoods in San Francisco to have underground power lines because above-ground power lines would obstruct the view. Everything ugly is hidden.

We know the high school boy who lives next door to me. He comes from a family that was prominent in the Gold Rush—I learned that from my California history textbooks. Photos of his parents frequently appear in the society pages of the *Nob Hill Gazette* that's delivered to our doorstep every month, free of charge. The boy is blond and often has a group of his high school friends over to watch football in his living room. From my garden I can see when they're watching a game. There's a three-foot gap between the edge of our property and his house and sometimes I leap through his open window and land on the floor of his living room. I am that daring. I am a daring enigma. I fantasize that one of them will invite me to the prom. And then one afternoon one of the boys grabs the waistband of my Guess? jeans. I try to get away, and I run in place for a moment like a cartoon character. The boys all laugh; I'm upset for days. I know that this gesture and their laughter mean they think of me as a little girl and not as a prospective prom date. After that their window is kept closed.

Then there are the Prospero boys, the sons of a doctor, who lived in my house before my family bought it. They are legendary. They are a cautionary tale. When my parents toured the house, the floor of what would become my bedroom was littered with beer bottles and needles. The windows were broken. When I talk to older boys and tell them I live in the Prospero boys' old house I get attention, and, I imagine, momentary respect. No one can believe what lunatics those boys were. Moms will shake their heads and say how sad it was, those boys, their father being a doctor and all.

The Prospero boys are the reason my parents were able to buy the house for the price they did. It was destroyed by these boys. No one else wanted to think their children would grow up to have parties and use needles and spray-paint obscenities on the walls of their own home. My father has always been able to look past the damaged lives a house has witnessed. That is his secret power. He grew up in a rented third-floor apartment on an alleyway in the Mission and, like many of his friends, had multiple jobs by the time he was fifteen. Newspaper-delivery boy, grocery-store employee, doorman at the Haight Theatre. He tore tickets six nights a week and on his day off he'd go see movies. When he was in middle school he biked all the way to Sea Cliff to go to the beach and he saw the majestic houses and said to his friends, "One day I will live in this neighborhood." One day he did. My mother grew up without money, too (she grew up in a large, happy family on a farm in rural Sweden), and together they are a thrifty pair—no meals out at restaurants, no heat turned on unless there's company, and sometimes no heat even then, just the strong smell of fish. My sister, Svea, who is ten, is the only one in our family who likes fish, but it is served weekly because we are Swedish.

In the front room of my house there are five large windows that look out on the Golden Gate Bridge. On foggy days the bridge is blanketed in white, no trace of it visible. On days like this, my father used to tell me that robbers had stolen the bridge. "Don't worry, Eulabee," he'd say to me, "the police are after them—they've been working all night." By midmorning when the fog began to burn off, he'd say, "Look, they got em! They're putting the bridge back." It was a story I never tired of, and reinforced two lessons that reigned over my childhood:

1.   Hard work conquers all obstacles.

2.   Good triumphs over evil (which is always lurking).

There are alerts, of course, and warnings, and in Sea Cliff these warnings come in the form of foghorns. First one foghorn, and in the distance, another. The deep bellowing foghorns are the soundtrack to my childhood. When we go to the beaches, which we often do, huddled in sweaters and with mist on our faces, the foghorns are even louder than they are in our houses. They punctuate our confessions, our laughter. We laugh a lot.

When I say "we," I sometimes mean the four of us Sea Cliff girls who are in the eighth grade at the Spragg School for Girls. But when I say "we," I always mean Maria Fabiola and me. Maria Fabiola is the oldest of three children—the youngest ones are twin boys. She moved to Sea Cliff the year we started kindergarten. Nobody knew much about her family. Sometimes she says she's part Italian. Other times she says she's not, why would you think that? Other times she says her grandfather was the prime minister of Italy. Or could have been prime minister. Or she was related to the mayor of Florence or could have been. She has long dark brown hair and light green eyes—even in black and white photos you can see their ethereal color. There are dozens of photos in her home of her and her cousins sitting atop horses, or on the edges of swimming pools surrounded by grass. The photos are taken by professionals and displayed in identical silver frames.

Maria Fabiola is a noticer, but also a laugher. She has a laugh that starts in her chest and comes out like a flute. She is known for her laugh because it's what people call a contagious laugh, but it's not contagious in the usual way. Hers is a laugh that makes you laugh because you don't want her to laugh alone. And she's beautiful. An older boy wearing corduroy OP shorts near Kezar Stadium once said she was hot and with any other girl we would call bullshit but with her we believe it—the compliment, the boy, the corduroy OP shorts.

She wears a thick stack of thin silver bracelets on her arm. We all wear these bracelets, which we buy on Haight Street (three for a dollar) or on Clement Street (five for a dollar) but she wears more of them. When she laughs her hair falls in front of her face and she sweeps it out of her eyes with her fingers, causing her bracelets to cascade up and down her arm. The sound of her bracelets is like her laughter: high-pitched and delicate, a waterfall of notes. She has perfect hair and always will.

When we were in kindergarten Maria Fabiola and I began walking to school together with older girls who went to Spragg. These girls would pick up Maria Fabiola at her house at the top of China Beach and wind their way up El Camino del Mar and collect me. Together, we'd walk the wide, well-paved street to pick up another girl who lives in the house that looks like a castle (it has a turret) and then continue to school.

The older girls passed down their knowledge of houses to us, and we combine this with the information we have from our parents. When we become the older girls at Spragg, we teach the younger girls about the houses, about who lives where, about which gardeners are pervy. From grades kindergarten until fourth we wear plaid green jumpers over white blouses with Peter Pan collars. In fifth grade through eighth grade we wear pleated blue skirts that stop right above the knee, and white sailor middies. It is the see-through white middies that provoke the gardeners' comments. "You are not so little anymore," they say, staring at our chests.

When we are thirteen Maria Fabiola and I walk with two other girls: Julia and Faith. Julia used to live a few houses up the street from me, in a home that looked like it could fall into the ocean. Her mom is a retired professional ice-skater with a wall of medals so Julia skates, too. Julia has shoulder-length light brown hair that shines blond in the sun and has blue eyes that she insists on calling "cobalt." She briefly dated a boy from Pacific Heights until one night on the phone she asked him what color her eyes were and he said "blue," and he was done for. Julia's half sister, Gentle, is seventeen. She's the daughter of Julia's father and his first wife, who was a hippie. Then Julia's father made money and the first wife couldn't stand the hypocrisy, so she left him and Gentle and moved to India. That's when Gentle's father married the ice-skater.

It's hard for Julia to have a half sister like Gentle. Gentle used to attend the Spragg School for Girls until she got kicked out. She goes to Grant, the public high school, which makes her one of the only people we know who goes there. The kids who go to Grant look huge and their coats are enormous. They give the finger to cops and even firemen. She used to babysit for me and Svea sometimes until my parents found out that one night, when I was eleven and she was fifteen, she taught me how to smoke.

Gentle has long tangled mouse-brown hair and wears bell-bottoms. She used to have hippie friends but now we usually see her alone. She's often drunk, stoned, on acid. Once we were at the playground by the golf course next to Spragg and we saw a crowd gathering and laughing at something. Julia, Maria Fabiola, and I went to see what it was and there was Gentle, naked and swinging from the monkey bars. Julia was furious. She ran home to tell her mom and didn't come to school the next day.

After a business scandal that was on the front page of the *Chronicle*, Julia's family had to move to a small house on the other side of California Street, beyond the border of Sea Cliff. They said they were only living there while doing construction on their main house, but I haven't seen any workers at their old house and I overheard my father tell my mother that he read in a real-estate report that it had been sold. Now they have no view of the ocean. Now they use their garage for a spare room and park their cars on the street. Between the scandal and having to move, we all feel bad for Julia, but we mostly feel bad for her because nobody would want a half sister like Gentle. My mom says she respects Julia's mom because it must be incredibly challenging to be a stepmother to such a lost girl. All the music Gentle likes is about drugs. Or the bands do drugs, or look like they do drugs. Everything about Gentle is grubby and unwashed but this is the eighties and the eighties are clean, and the colors are bright and separated.

Then there's Faith. She's one of us. Faith moved to San Francisco last year in seventh grade, and lives in a house that extends an entire block on Sea View. She has long red hair that on some days makes her look like Anne of Green Gables, and on other days like Pippi Longstocking. She plays goalie on the soccer team and is always diving for the ball, her hair streaming behind her like a flag. She has this air about her like she knows she's special, and maybe it's because she resembles famous literary characters or maybe it's because she's adopted. Her father is a lot younger than her mother. They had a daughter but she died and so they adopted Faith to replace her. The dead daughter's name was Faith, too, which I think is strange and Julia thinks is horrendous because her favorite word is "horrendous." But Faith doesn't mind that she was named after the dead daughter. In fact, sometimes she says she feels like she's twenty because the original Faith lived to be seven and Faith is now thirteen. I don't know what Faith's mom was like before the original Faith died, but she now acts like life is a large broken car she's pushing down the road. She walks diagonally, as though she's making her way through a rainstorm, even on the fairest of days.

The four of us—Maria Fabiola, Faith, Julia, and I—own these streets of Sea Cliff, but it's Maria Fabiola and I who know the beaches the best. Maybe it's because our houses are closest to the shore. Her house is situated above China Beach and mine is just up the street—a four-minute walk.

We take the boys from Sea View to the beach and under their gaze we see how agile we are. We can feel our power as we race on all fours over the cliffs—we know their crevices and footholds, their smooth inclines and their rugged patches. If there were an Olympic category for climbing these cliffs, we would enter it; we scale them as though we are in training. After an afternoon at the beach, the pads of our fingers are rough, and our palms smell of damp rock, and the boys are dazzled.

China Beach is adjacent to a bigger beach, Baker Beach, and they're separated by a promontory, but Maria Fabiola and I know how to traverse between the two beaches at low tide. We know how to read the ocean, how to navigate the slippery rocks so that if we time it perfectly we can wait until the ocean starts to inhale its waves and, through a combination of climbing and scurrying, make our way to Baker Beach. Once, on a class outing to China Beach, we knew the tide was right to make a mad dash around the bluff and end up at Baker. Other classmates followed us. When our teachers yelled for us to come back, Maria Fabiola and I timed the waves and ran. Our classmates didn't know the beach the way we did, hesitated, and got stuck on the other side. The teachers panicked. We assured them it would be okay. We climbed over the bluff and held our classmates' hands, watched the ocean, and guided our classmates back to China Beach. We tried to remain humble but we were heroes.

2

Maria Fabiola and I have been best friends since we were in kindergarten at Spragg, and we have been placed in different homerooms almost every year. Separately we are good girls. We behave. Together, some strange alchemy occurs and we are trouble. This happens at school, and it happens when we're not at school. Last year I got into trouble with my parents and with my neighbors for telling a lie that involved her. Maria Fabiola and I were selling lemonade. We weren't getting many customers in front of my house, so we moved our stand in front of a bigger one on a corner. A Chevy full of teenage boys pulled up, and the boy in the passenger seat leaned out the window to talk to us. "If that's your house, can we marry you when you're older?"

Maria Fabiola and I looked at each other and laughed. We didn't correct their assumption.

"We'll take that as a yes," the boy said. As the car drove off, he yelled out the window, "We'll be back!" To some, that might sound like a threat, but to us it was a promise.

Mrs. Sheridan, a neighbor I'd known most of my life, was our first customer. "What do we have here today, Eulabee?"

"Lemonade," I said, pointing to the sign that said "Lemonade."

She bought one cup, which she drank on the spot, and then bought a second. "And what's your name?" she said to Maria Fabiola.

"Maria Fabiola."

I would have thought Mrs. Sheridan might recognize her from all the times she'd been at my house, but apparently not. Her non-recognition of Maria Fabiola made me look at my friend differently. And for the first time I saw what everyone else must be seeing: she was no longer who she used to be. Her hair, once straight, had become wavy. Her body had swelled, stretching the fabric of her shirt and the back pockets of her jeans, so now the pockets tilted inward toward each other at an angle. The lie flew out of my mouth, a fabrication intended to collapse the distance spreading between us. "Maria Fabiola's not just my friend," I said to Mrs. Sheridan. "My parents recently adopted her. She's my new sister."

Mrs. Sheridan, who wore a large cross on a thin chain around her neck, thought this was wonderful news. I did, too. It was hard, at first, to see what Maria Fabiola thought of my lie—her full lips were pillowed together into a pout—but she began to repeat the fib, and then embrace it, and this pleased me. We proceeded to walk around the block, ringing the doorbells and knocking the knockers and I introduced Maria Fabiola to every neighbor as my new adopted sister.

We rang a few more doorbells, almost all of which were answered. Did no one in Sea Cliff work? Each neighbor accepted our lie as truth. The ease of deception made the lying less fun, so we stopped and returned to my house to get a snack. We made ants on a log—peanut butter on celery with raisins on top.

"I didn't know you were such a good liar," Maria Fabiola said. She seemed to be evaluating me with new eyes.

"I didn't either," I said.

We continued eating without talking, the snap of the celery the only noise.

Maria Fabiola's mom came to pick her up in her black Volvo. Her mother had dark hair and wore large sunglasses so opaque that sometimes it appeared she had difficulty seeing through the lenses. She often lifted them up in an attempt to get a better view, and then let them fall back over her eyes as though disappointed at what things really looked like. She quickly whisked Maria Fabiola away. I hoped nobody saw her leave. Maria Fabiola's departure had no part in the narrative of my newly fabricated family life.

It wasn't long before the phone started ringing. Neighbors were calling to congratulate my parents on the new addition to our family, and to ask if we needed help with the transition. Hand-me-down clothes, food, anything at all.

During the phone calls, my parents were very attentive and intrigued. I couldn't see their faces because I was hiding in the hall closet, standing inside a long raccoon fur coat that belonged to my mother. I knew the inside of this coat well. Its lining had a complicated brown and black and white pattern, into which my mother's initials—G.S.—had been stitched and camouflaged. I had been told that if anyone ever stole the coat, she would be able to identify it as hers by pointing out the initials, but it was never explained to me why anyone would want to steal the coat and I never saw my mom wear it outside of the house—or in the house, either. Even the raccoon coat couldn't muffle the sounds of my parents' voices; I could hear they were befuddled, and angry. The closet door was opened. I had been hiding inside the long raccoon fur coat since I was little so it was not such a good hiding place, really. Five minutes later I was retracing my steps around the neighborhood, ringing cold doorbells and apologizing to stern faces.

3

My dad comes home one day in September and says that an episode of a TV show I haven't heard of is going to be filmed at Joseph & Joseph. Joseph & Joseph is the art and antique gallery he owns on the other side of town. My father's name is Joseph and when he was coming up with the logo he wanted an ampersand because he thought it looked more impressive. One small setback: he didn't have a partner, so just repeated his own name. Now an episode of a not-well-known detective show is going to be filmed at the gallery and my dad has asked if Svea, my friends, and I want to be in the establishing shot. I don't know what an establishing shot is, but I call Maria Fabiola, Faith, and Julia, and we plan what we're going to wear.

We're disappointed when we learn that whoever's in charge wants us to wear our school uniforms.

My father's antique gallery is South of Market. He found a small block he liked so he went door to door and offered cash to each of the owners of the houses. A couple of the owners remembered my dad from when he was a kid delivering newspapers. They were happy to take the cash; they were happy to leave. Then my father built Joseph & Joseph. The gallery hasn't changed the neighborhood much—outside its large French doors, men sit drinking straight from the bottle. But once you step inside Joseph & Joseph, it feels like you're in a giant dollhouse.

Two floors of the building are filled with antiques. There's also an auction room, which is often rented out for parties. My father has photos of himself with O.J. Simpson, with Mayor Dianne Feinstein. In the photo I can see her beautiful legs. My dad talks a lot about Dianne Feinstein's legs. Once, after describing them, he said "Yowzah."

My favorite thing in the gallery is a Chinese spice cabinet. It's almost six feet tall and four feet wide, and has forty-two drawers that are deep and long. I love opening a drawer and inhaling and trying to guess what spice was stored there. Then I close the drawer and open the next one. It's like a library card catalog for smells.

My father has a secretary named Arlene. Arlene is the sister of my dad's best friend from their days growing up in the alley. My dad is loyal to his friends from the neighborhood. Arlene's hair is so long it extends past her belt, and she's partial to blouses with ties and burgundy pants. She can be grumpy sometimes and I know this means that it's her time of the month. I first learned this from my dad and I hate that he knows this. I hate that I know this. I keep a chart in my calendar of when she's grumpy toward me on the phone or in person, and it tracks: she's testy toward me every four weeks.

At other times she's sweet and attentive. She gives me baby aspirin when I have a headache, and she lets me touch all the antiques, even the indoor marble fountain with the naked angel balanced precariously on top. The water spouts from the angel's mouth like projectile vomit.

On the day of the filming my mother drives Svea, Maria Fabiola, Faith, Julia, and me to the gallery after school. She has brought me a new, freshly pressed uniform, but this embarrasses me, so I don't change into it. But Maria Fabiola, who spilled mustard on her uniform that day at lunch, says she'd like to use it.

When we get to the gallery, half the furniture has been moved to make way for lights and cameras. My spice cabinet hasn't been touched. Arlene has ironed her hair so it's exceptionally straight today, and my dad is wearing his silver tie, his best tie, even though he's not going to be on camera.

Maria Fabiola takes the hanger with my newly pressed blue uniform skirt and my white middy into the bathroom and changes. When she comes out, I can't help but stare. The middy, which is loose on me, is tight on her. I usually wear a white T-shirt under my middy but she's not wearing one. Nor is she wearing a bra.

The director, who isn't dressed up at all and doesn't have a director's chair (a disappointment) tells us it's time for the establishing shot. We go outside the building and see a camera has been set up. Faith, Julia, Svea, Maria Fabiola, and I are supposed to skip in front of the gallery like we're heading home from school. It occurs to me that we were instructed to wear our uniforms because this will make it look like the gallery is in an upscale part of town, a part of the city where there are private schools. The reality is that there aren't any private schools within walking distance of Joseph & Joseph.

We skip in front of the entranceway in one direction. Then we walk back to the starting point and skip again.

After the third take the director talks to an assistant and the assistant talks to my dad and then my dad whispers with my mom. I watch their mouths moving but can't make out what they're saying. Finally my mom comes over to me and my friends. "This time, girls, let's try it without the skipping. Oh, and Maria Fabiola, the director doesn't want everyone looking so similar. Can you put on your uniform sweater?" Maria Fabiola does as instructed and then we walk in front of the gallery two more times.

"And . . . cut!" the director yells. He doesn't use a megaphone, but still my friends and I find it exciting that he's using official movie language.

We're thanked and told this episode of the show won't air for a few months, but not even this delay can dampen our moods. My mom drives us home, and we're all hyper, including Svea, who's happy because my friends are paying attention to her and Faith's even braiding her pretty hair.

That night in the kitchen I ask my mother what the whispering on set was about. "Oh, that," my mother says. "I don't remember."

"Yes, you do," I say.

"Well, don't tell your friends, but the director thought that Maria Fabiola's appearance was distracting."

"Distracting?"

"That's the word he used," my mother says.

"Huh," I say, trying to act casual.

That night, I do a two-way call and I inform Julia and Maria Fabiola that the director thought Maria Fabiola was "distracting." Maria Fabiola starts laughing and I join her. Julia is silent and then tries to act like she's not the slightest bit jealous.

"Sorry I wasn't laughing before," Julia says, "but I was *distracted.*"

I hear Maria Fabiola's bracelets jingling and I know she's running her fingers through her long, long hair.

4

I am at Faith's house the night her father kills him-self. All four of us are there. It's Faith's birthday and we go to the Alexandria Theatre on Geary to watch *The Breakfast Club*. We watch the movie with rapt attention and with glee. When we leave the theater we are delirious. "Don't you forget about me," we say to each other over and over again. We want all the boys from the film to pay attention to us. We want to want. We want to love. We want to want love. We are on the precipice of having real boyfriends, of making out with them. We know this. We can feel this urge pulsating through our bodies, but we don't know what to call it—we won't call it desire—or how to express it to each other or to ourselves. And so we continue to laugh and sing "Don't you forget about me" until

Faith's mother arrives at the theater in a ridiculous red raincoat, made more ridiculous by the fact that it's not raining. She puts her finger to her lips and says, "Shhh."

Faith's birthday dinner is at Al's Place on Clement Street. Faith's father, who is handsome and at least a dozen years younger than Faith's mom, joins us after work. He orders a steak and what on TV they call a stiff drink. Faith's mother orders a diet soft drink, which she sips through a straw, from which she hasn't successfully removed the paper wrapper. A piece of white paper sticks to her lip for half the meal. When she excuses herself to use the restroom, Faith's father orders another stiff drink. Faith's father asks us each a few questions and tries hard to get my name and Julia's name straight. He remembers Maria Fabiola's name easily. Everyone remembers Maria Fabiola. Her looks have recently become troublingly arresting. Her body has blossomed more, and this has gifted her face an expression of constant surprise, as though even she can't believe her good fortune.

We return to Faith's house after dinner and a sad slice of cake. Faith gives us a tour because Maria Fabiola hasn't been inside before. "Never?" Julia asks. "I have a lot of after-school activities," Maria Fabiola replies. She and I have the same number of after-school activities.

We started taking ballet together at the Olenska School of Ballet when puberty began to take over our bodies, making us clumsy and laminating our curves with fat. Not that our instructor, Madame Sonya, thinks there's much hope for us—she often quotes Isadora Duncan, who said that American bodies aren't made for ballet. Still, while the dance classes haven't done much for me, they have helped define Maria Fabiola's figure. In addition to ballet, we go to dancing school every other Wednesday. All of us at Spragg go to ballroom dancing school because that's where you meet the boys who go to the all-boys' schools.

Faith's house is decorated with Laura Ashley patterns—tiny pastel flowers on white curtains, tiny pastel flowers on tablecloths, tiny pastel flowers everywhere. The house is clearly bigger than their home in Connecticut was because their furniture can't fill all the spaces. And so it's the kind of house that has a couch in one room, a desk in another. I know Maria Fabiola isn't getting the full tour because Faith's parents are home. The full tour includes the stack of *Playboy*s her dad keeps in a shoebox in his closet, along with a gun— "the gun's just to scare burglars," according to Faith. The full tour includes the piles of pathetic diaries her mother keeps under her side of the bed. Each page lists what she's eaten on a particular day and rates her intake as good or bad. The diaries never detail anything else about her days besides her food consumption.

Without the prolonged stop in her parents' bedroom, the tour doesn't last very long. After five minutes we end up back in the kitchen and start making popcorn. I look around—suddenly Maria Fabiola isn't with us. Faith's mom asks if we want to run to the corner store to buy Virgina Slims. She often sends Faith to the store with money and a note giving her permission to buy cigarettes. "Not on my birthday!" Faith yells. Her mom picks up her stained purse with its long fraying strap and leaves to get them herself. We don't end up eating the popcorn because it's burnt.

A cool saltwater breeze enters the house and we follow it through the open back door and into the garden. Faith's father is outside in the dim light having a drink. He's sitting on a short white bench that I realize is a swing. It's the kind of swing that you see in musicals or plays set in the South. Seated next to him on the swing is Maria Fabiola.

"Let's ride the elevator," Faith calls out.

"I'm speaking with your friend, Faith," her father says.

"It only fits three anyway," Faith says, with an accusatory glance at Maria Fabiola. Then Julia and I follow Faith inside. The walls of the elevator are decorated with long ribbons that have been stapled at the top and the bottom. There's an assortment of colors like those at Baskin Robbins: strawberry, pistachio, banana, and mandarin. "The previous owner decorated it like this," Faith explains, though it's evident that the frivolity of fluttering ribbons is antithetical to her mother's entire being, which might be why we had to wait until she left to enter the elevator. We ride up and down and up and down the four stories of the house until I feel claustrophobic. When I get out on the bottom floor, Maria Fabiola is coming in from the garden, wearing an expression I can't decipher.

"How was the elevator ride?" she asks, in a condescending voice.

"Honestly," I say, looking at her, "I feel kind of sick."

Faith's mother returns home, and the four of us girls seclude ourselves in Faith's room, also covered in little flowers. Her books (few in number, and young for our grade) are too neatly aligned between white bookends that are meant to resemble owls but look more like melted moons. On her floor is a circular shag rug, and we run our fingers through its long, cloud-colored fibers like we're stroking blades of grass in heaven.

We study Faith's yearbooks from her school in Darien, Connecticut. In particular, we study the boys who were her classmates and the boys who were a year above her and rate them on a scale of one to four stars. We ask Faith about the cuter ones—are they funny? What music do they like? Do they play lacrosse?—as though her answers will help determine whether or not they are worthy of a crush. This is how it is for us at an all-girls' school in Sea Cliff—the objects of our affection are either projected on a movie screen or else encapsulated by a square-inch photo from a yearbook in Connecticut. After an hour of flipping through the yearbook, each of us exclaiming "Mine!" when we see a boy we like, Faith aggressively shuts the yearbook and returns it to the shelf, next to the strange, sad owl.

When Faith's mother tells us it's time to go to bed, we change for sleep. Faith removes a Laura Ashley nightgown from a hanger in her closet, then closes the closet door so she can change in privacy. Julia turns her back to the rest of us and slips on an ice-skating T-shirt with silver sequins on the skate's blades. She keeps her bra on when she sleeps because she thinks this will help ensure her breasts are perky when she's older. I turn to a different corner and remove my off-white bra and pull on dark blue pajama bottoms and a Hello Kitty T-shirt that I hope everyone will know I'm wearing ironically. When I turn back around I see

Maria Fabiola lifting her shirt up above her chest. She hasn't bothered to hide her body. Over the summer she's grown full breasts that look like great scoops of ice cream. I see Julia trying not to stare. I try not to stare. Maria Fabiola pulls on a thin hot pink T-shirt that's tight across the chest. It depicts two angels, one blond and one dark-haired, wearing sunglasses. I have permission, I figure, to study her chest when trying to read the word written in cursive beneath the cherub's faces: "Fiorucci."

We unroll our sleeping bags on the rug, each of us trying to position our bags next to Maria Fabiola. We stay up talking about *The Breakfast Club* and deciding which one of us would date which boy. Then we giggle until Faith's father roars at us to be quiet. "Don't you forget about me," we repeat to each other in whispers until, like candles being extinguished one at a time, each of us drops into sleep.

In the middle of the night I'm awakened by shrieks. They're so loud I assume they're coming from one of my friends. But after sitting up I understand they're coming from another bedroom, and that it's Faith's mother screaming. Faith jumps up and switches on the light and runs to her parents' room. Julia, Maria Fabiola, and I look at each other, dazed. Then we hear Faith shrieking, too.

Her father shot himself. The ambulance arrives and two efficient and menacing men carry him both carefully and recklessly through the house on a stretcher. The stretcher hits the wall as they turn down the circular staircase, a lamp is knocked over and splintered into shards, and Faith's mother swears. Faith pulls on a sweater and pants. She grabs her mother's jacket from the hall closet. We tell each other we are in the way and retreat to Faith's room.

The front door shuts so heavily the house shudders, and the men's booming footsteps are no more. We peer out of the room and soon realize Faith is gone, too. The sirens of the ambulance fade into the night and the three of us girls sit shattered in Faith's room, our sleeping bags lying inertly on the floor like discarded cocoons. Maria Fabiola starts to cry, first silently while physically convulsing. And then, as though the motions of her body are like a pump at a well, her sobs begin to emerge in short bursts. Then they start to undulate. The drama is overwhelming. Julia and I call our parents, and then call Maria Fabiola's parents for her.

My father arrives, still dressed in a suit from an art auction. Julia's mother arrives in a tight-fitting zip-up sweatshirt that says "Ice Queen," and Maria Fabiola's mother arrives in a silk bathrobe. None of us knows if we should leave and lock the front door. What if Faith's mother doesn't have a key? What if Faith comes back and needs us? So we sit huddled around the kitchen table as though we're playing an invisible game of cards. The mothers turn toward my father, who I'm sure can feel their attention. He initiates a prayer, something he rarely does, to calm everyone down. We all hold hands around the kitchen table and close our eyes. I peek and see that while my father's eyelids are still shut as he leads the prayer, both Maria Fabiola's and Julia's mother's eyes are open, looking anxiously toward him.

5

After the funeral (a recognizable local politician in the second row, soggy cucumber sandwiches at the reception), the four of us become like paper dolls—we are always together, connected. At school we play four square or else tetherball with two people per team. We don't welcome anyone to join us and the teachers permit us to be exclusive—they have Faith's best interest at heart.

At Faith's house there are constant visitors coming from the East Coast to offer their condolences and help. When they depart, they leave meals in Faith's freezer, which her mother promptly throws away. At Julia's house her parents sell one Mercedes and then another. At Maria Fabiola's house they get a new burglar alarm put in after their surveillance camera catches some unsavory behavior behind the house. Maria Fabiola's father won't tell his children what, exactly, the surveillance camera picked up.

At my house, everything continues as usual. My mother starts work early—she bikes to the hospital at 6 a.m. for the morning nursing shift so she can be home with Svea and me in the afternoon. My father gets us ready for school and makes us oatmeal, which Svea eats while sketching a new fire station. She says she wants to be an architect when she grows up and is often hunched over her sketches with a ruler and a blue pencil.

On a morning like any other, Svea's chubby and dour friend rings the bell. She and Svea head to school together—they follow a direct route up El Camino del Mar. A few minutes later, Maria Fabiola climbs the brick steps to our house. I say goodbye to my dad, who has tissue stuck to his face from where he cut himself shaving. I want to remove the tissue, to hug him goodbye, but my friend is watching, waiting. Together Maria Fabiola and I walk out of Sea Cliff to pick up Julia.

Julia's mom opens the door and right away I smell something burning. Julia's mom must see me sniffing. "Gentle bought some new incense," she says and smiles at me and then at Maria Fabiola. "I have an idea," she says, as Julia comes to the door. "Let's take a photo of you girls." She retrieves her camera and the three of us line up, Maria Fabiola is in the middle. Julia and I stare at each other as the shutter closes. We both know Maria Fabiola's recent transformation from ordinary to otherworldly beauty inspires everyone to want to capture it.

"You girls look great," Julia's mom says, not looking at me.

"Bye, mom," Julia says, closing the door. The fresh air is a relief. We make our way to Faith's house. Faith lives a block and a half from school but we still pick her up every morning. We do anything for Faith.

"You think Faith's mom is ever going to get re-married?" Maria Fabiola asks, her bracelets jingling as she moves her backpack from one shoulder to the other.

"My parents think she's too homely to find someone new," Julia says matter-of-factly. "And my mom is my dad's second wife, so they know about these things."

"It's probably way too soon for her to date anyone else," I say firmly, as though I have authority on these matters.

"Maybe we could help her pick out some new clothes," Julia says. "She needs a fashion overhaul."

"Totally," Maria Fabiola says. "Also, don't you think the teachers are being easy on Faith?"

"Of course they are," I say. "They should be."

"I have a cousin," Julia says, "who said that at her college they have a rule there that if your roommate dies, you automatically get As for the semester."

"That's not such a good rule," Maria Fabiola says. "I mean, wouldn't it just encourage you to drive your roommate to kill herself?"

We cross the street and pass by a parked, old-fashioned white car at the crosswalk. We notice a man sitting inside. The car window is rolled down and the man, who is older than we are but younger than our fathers, asks us for the time.

I check my Swatch watch—why is it ticking so loudly?—and tell him it's just after eight in the morning.

"Thank you," he says. "I thought it was later." My friends and I continue walking.

"Did you see that?" Maria Fabiola says.

Julia looks hesitantly at Maria Fabiola. "Yes," she says. Then, "Yes!"

"What?" I ask.

"He was touching himself," Maria Fabiola says.

Julia looks at Maria Fabiola for a minute. "He was. That's right."

"What?" I say.

"Didn't you see?" Julia says.

"He was stroking it the whole time," Maria Fabiola says.

"Stroking what?" I say.

"His PENIS! And he said he's going to find us later!" Maria Fabiola says.

"Yes, later, he said later!" Julia rushes to add.

We reach Faith's house—two blocks away from where the car was parked—and Maria Fabiola and Julia tell Faith their version of what happened. Julia repeats what Maria Fabiola has already said, and Maria Fabiola adds new details. Faith shrieks a shriek that's a mix of delight and horror.

"This is going to be such a big deal," Maria Fabiola says.

"I swear I didn't see anything strange," I say.

"Oh, is that an everyday experience for you?" Julia says. "Penis-stroking in white cars?" Maria Fabiola laughs.

My friends tease me for not having seen anything, for not having heard anything, and then they start ignoring me. Even Faith, who wasn't present at the time of the incident in question, is offended. Fueled by elated indignation, my three friends run ahead to school.

I lag behind and then stop. I feel like I'm on a boat tilting over in the wind—someone needs to leap to the other side to balance the weight. Maria Fabiola started the lie, Julia parroted everything she said, and now Faith believes them. I walk the last half block to school by myself.

Shortly after arriving at school, my homeroom teacher tells me I'm being summoned to Mr. Makepeace's office. Mr. Makepeace—his real name—is the headmaster and he's from England. His British accent and his framed degrees from Cambridge put all the parents at ease. I have never been summoned to his office before.

I walk all the way across campus, past each of the classrooms I've occupied over the years. I pass the sculpture of Ms. Spragg, the wealthy woman whom the school is named after. She was pretty, if the statue is an accurate representation of her appearance, and her beauty has not gone unnoticed. The statue is bronze and her breasts and her right hand have been polished silver by repeated touches.

I pass the bushes where butterflies like to flutter and feed. Sometimes we catch them in jars for a minute before releasing them. Sometimes we wait too long to release them and find them dead. We know the names of the girls who keep the butterflies too long, and we have no idea what to do with this information.

I am a very good student with a sinister side and I'm not sure how much Mr. Makepeace knows about this side. I wonder if the headmaster knows that occasionally I count how many times the new Australian P.E. teacher, Mr. Robinson, says "Understand?" when he's explaining the rules of a game. Then, when Mr. Robinson's finished talking, and asks if we have any questions, I raise my hand and say, "Do you realize you said 'Understand' thirty-one times?" This makes him ballistic and he lectures me in front of the class. During the lecture his Australian accent intensifies and he says, "Don't ever count my words. Understand?" This makes all my classmates laugh and makes him more ballistic.

Mr. Makepeace's secretary, Ms. Patel—the mother of the only two Indian girls in the school—stands up when I enter the front office and says, "Good morning, Eulabee." She usually calls me "Eula" or "Bee" but today she is formal and asks me to take a seat and wait for my turn. Maria Fabiola emerges from Mr. Makepeace's office looking radiant, like she's an opera singer who's just gotten a standing ovation. "Stick to the story," Maria Fabiola whispers into my ear before Ms. Patel instructs her to return to her classroom. Then Ms. Patel leads me into Mr. Makepeace's office, which has a large photo of the headmasters' three sons in British school uniforms. It reeks of cigar though I've never seen Mr. Makepeace smoke. Two police officers sit uncomfortably in chairs that are typically reserved for sets of prospective parents or those parents who are being informed their daughter would do better else-where. They are chairs of transition.

I'm introduced to the officers and they ask me to describe what happened that morning. I tell them it had been a walk like any other. I tell them exactly where the car was parked. One of the officers scrib-bles notes in a little notebook. They ask me what happened with the man.

"He asked us for the time," I say.

"And then what?"

"I told him the time. It was a few minutes after eight."

"What did he say?"

"He said he thought it was later."

"He thought it was later? That's what he said?"

"Yes."

"Did he suggest he'd find you or your friends later?"

"No."

"Did he do anything inappropriate?"

"I didn't see anything inappropriate."

"Nothing?"

"Nothing."

"What did the car look like?"

"It was white, vintage. The window was down."

"Was the door open?"

"The door was closed."

"What happened after you gave him the time?"

"We turned and kept walking to school."

"And that was it?"

"That's when my friends said they had seen something. But I was confused."

"Why were you confused?"

"Because I didn't see anything."

The headmaster thanks me, the police officers thank me. I wonder if they're disappointed or relieved.

I leave the room and its cigar smoke, which clings to my hair. Waiting in the front office is Julia, who is about to be called. I don't make eye contact with her but instead stare at her white K-Swiss sneakers.

That evening my parents ask about the encounter. The school has called them, of course. Mr. Makepeace has told them the cops aren't going to pursue any action. He and the police believe my version of the morning's events.

They believe *me*.

6

My mother skips aerobics that evening. I know things are serious when she skips aerobics. I joined her a few times at a middle school gym on Arguello and was startled by how many friends she had in the class. A muscular woman with an attached microphone danced energetically on a stage while almost a hundred women of all sizes faced her and mimicked her moves. The women wore leotards over leggings and at the end of the class they got down on the dusty floor and did leg lifts. I saw the wet stains around the women's groins and I felt embarrassed for them, for myself, for the plight of women.

Instead of going to aerobics tonight, my mother cleans the already clean floors of the dining room.

"You know how this all started, don't you?" she says.

"With a man in the car," I say. I'm sitting in a dining-room chair. We only sit in this room for holiday meals or when we have company.

"No," she says, and she wrings out her rag in the square white plastic bin she occasionally uses to soak her feet after a long nursing shift. She is on all fours and has one damp rag in her hand and another dry one under her knees. The floors are wooden and hard, and she needs the old rag, its texture bumpy like cottage cheese, to protect her. Most of my friends' parents hire cleaning people. That's what happens when you own a house in our neighborhood—you have cleaning people. But not my parents. They don't believe in hiring people. Especially not cleaning people. Not when my mother can clean better than anyone.

She moves her rag to the right and then replaces her knees on top of it and continues to clean. "This is all because of those parent lectures they started at school last spring. The first speaker was this woman from Stanford." My mother touches her nose and I know this means she's saying this woman was stuck-up. Someone else might think she's gesturing that this woman was a pig, but my mother grew up on a farm and doesn't insult animals.

"This woman who came from Stanford"—she says it like Stan-fjord—"she said that she was going to share with us the secret to raising successful girls."

"Really?" Like all thirteen-year-old girls I find the word *secret* intriguing.

"She said we should never tell our daughters they were beautiful. According to her, this was a terrible idea. And so of course every family has been following her advice because she's a professor at . . ." My mother doesn't even say the university's name, she just presses her palm against her nose. "But since that day, all you girls have been seeking attention. You've all been looking in the mirror, wondering if you're pretty. When I was growing up, we didn't even have mirrors. We only had a lake."

With that, she stands up, ventures into the kitchen, and returns with a bottle of Windex. She begins spraying the glass of the antique mirror with the gold frame. The mirror is from my dad's antique gallery. Our entire house looks like the gallery, and I often wonder if it would have been furnished differently if my parents had had a boy. With girls you can keep fragile things.

I have a hard time focusing on my homework. I call my friends and leave messages for them. No one calls me back.

———————

The next day I walk to school by myself—the other girls get rides from their parents. I pass the spot where the car was parked. It's empty now. I stare at it as though it's an archaeological site of historical significance. Then I turn and continue my walk to school, alone. In my locker I find a folded note addressed to Benedict Arnold, but his name's been crossed out and my name's been written on top. The note contains one word: "Traiter!" Maria Fabiola has always been a terrible speller.

In homeroom, I think even the teacher, Ms. Livesey, is looking at me strangely. Ms. Livesey lives in Berkeley, a world away. We know a lot about her because she's one of the few teachers who talks about her life outside the classroom. She paints women with artichokes or avocadoes or guavas over their private parts, and sometimes she shows us slides of her "work in progress." Last year she brought her twenty-one-year-old son in to talk to us about his time in the Peace Corps. She wears her black hair messy—not uncombed enough to elicit complaints from the parents, but just tousled enough to suggest she spent the night in the woods. We wonder if she shaves her armpits. We assume people in Berkeley don't shave. Sometimes she has splatters of paint on her shoes and we know she's been working on her canvases. It excites us to know she has passions beyond us, her students. It thrills us that her son is cute.

Sometimes classmates like to sit near my desk so they can cheat off my quizzes, but today no one wants to sit next to me. Ms. Livesey hands out a xeroxed form with nine squares on it. It's a questionnaire intended to help us determine what level of information we would give out to a stranger, what we would tell a friend, what we would tell a family member. Clearly, it's not a coincidence that this worksheet is being distributed for discussion today. The sheet is intended for an older audience—in the center is a box that says: "Things You Would Not Even Tell Yourself." Ms. Livesey has Xed out the box, which of course only serves to make it more intriguing. What, I wonder, would I not tell myself?

Next is science. It's our third day of the sex ed unit. On the first day our teacher passed around pads and tampons and told us to never douche because it interferes with the body's natural ecosystem. On the second day we watched a VHS recording of a young woman giving birth without pain medication. (The woman was white and preppy and looked like she could have gone to Spragg.) We all covered our eyes and vowed to never have children.

The science teacher is named Ms. McGilly and we call her Ms. Mc., which she doesn't particularly like. She doesn't particularly like us either. She's bone-thin with straight, gray-red hair, has a son our age and two young daughters who she's told us she would never send to Spragg. We know she won't be around long. She'll go the way our music teacher went after she taught us the song "Little Boxes." We liked our music teacher, who let us call her by her first name, Jane. She wore Western-style belts and brushed her brown hair in front of us until it glistened. (Ms. Mc. told us it was a disgrace to brush one's hair in public.) One day Jane said to the class: "Don't you get it? You girls in your uniforms and your nice houses are like the little boxes in the song. You're all the same. They're stripping you of your individuality." That was the last we saw of Jane. For months we thought it was because she'd used the word "stripping."

Today Ms. Mc. is passing around contraceptives. First a condom, which everyone decides smells terrible, then spermicide with an applicator, which is fun to slide up and down like a Push-Up ice cream treat, then a diaphragm that looks like a pink trampoline for a rodent. Next are the birth control pills. The orderliness of the packet—all the pills lined up perfectly in four rows of seven—reminds me of what Jane said about us all being identical. I punch out three of the pills and slip them into the pocket of my shorts. We all wear shorts under our blue skirts for P.E. class, when we drop our uniforms on the sidelines of the field or on the bleachers of the gym.

I spend recess in the library, and lunch alone in the cafeteria with the book I've checked out. I've read the book before but today I need the reassurance of a familiar plot. I wait for someone to sit next to me at the rectangular table, or for someone to talk to me as they pass by, but no one does. Across the cafeteria I see Maria Fabiola laughing. Even though she's far away I know what her bracelets sound like as they spiral up and down her tan arm.

A lunch without friends is a lunch that's too long. I glance at my Swatch watch frequently, and at one point am convinced it's stopped though it's still ticking as loudly as a guilty heartbeat. Through the pleated fabric of my skirt, I pat the pocket of my shorts, searching for the pills—I'm not sure what their purpose is. They're like tiny Easter eggs I've collected. What does anyone do with Easter eggs except show off how many have been found, and then let them rot?

Toward the end of the lunch period, I'm scheduled to meet with Mr. London, the English teacher, to discuss the extra-credit reading he's recommended for me. Mr. London came to Spragg soon after graduating college and he's probably too young to be teaching eighth graders—there's not enough of an age gap. At the start of the school year Mr. London assigned Jack London's work, and someone asked if he was related to Jack London. He became theatrically vague about whether he might be related to the great writer, which didn't fool me. Other students at the school like to make connections between things that have no roots in reality.

We meet in the Male Teacher's Lounge, which is basically his private office because there are no other male teachers except for the P.E. teacher, Mr. Robinson, who uses the Sports Staff office as his lair. He even put an Australian flag on the door to mark his territory. The Female Teacher's Lounge is crowded and smells like the shallow vase water of dying flowers. The Male Teacher's Lounge always smells of burnt coffee—the scent of testosterone, I assume.

Today Mr. London and I are meeting to discuss *Franny and Zooey*. He sits back in his desk chair and strokes his clean-shaven chin. Behind him, on three shelves, are books by Hemingway (*The Sun Also Rises, A Moveable Feast*), Fitzgerald (*Tender Is the Night*), and Robert Louis Stevenson (*Kidnapped*). There's also an entire shelf devoted to the work of

Jack London, which I personally believe he's included in his "library" to subliminally propel the myth that he's related to Jack London without having to prove it.

"So, what did you think of the book?" Mr. London says.

"What?" I say, still staring at the volumes on his shelves.

"*Franny and Zooey?*"

"Right," I say. "I didn't like it."

"What do you mean you didn't like it?" Mr. London asks.

"I mean that I liked *Catcher in the Rye,* but *Franny and Zooey* . . . well, it was okay."

"It was okay?" he says. "Salinger is okay?"

"Yes," I tell him. "I'd give the book a B minus."

"Then I'm afraid I'm going to have to give you a B minus," Mr. London says.

"For extra credit?"

"Don't you know that Salinger is an icon? That he's a genius?" he says.

"It doesn't mean I have to think this book is good," I say.

"Yes, it does," Mr. London says, clenching his youthful jaw.

"Why?" I ask.

"It's a masterpiece," Mr. London says, standing up.

"I thought it was boring," I say. "I think I'm the ideal audience and I didn't care for it. I wouldn't recommend it to anyone."

"You wouldn't recommend it to anyone," he says. He starts pacing the narrow room. I know what's about to happen. Any minute now he's going to jump through a window. Mr. London has a well-documented temper problem. Well-documented by me at least. Every time he's had a meltdown in the classroom I've reported it to Ms. Catanese, the upper school headmistress. She's an uptight onetime beauty with long legs and short skirts and high-collared blouses, who was extremely interested in the information I shared with her. I don't think Mr. London knows it was me who reported him. Others, I've been told, have complained about his temper as well. But it was Ms. Catanese who told me this so when she says others have complained about his temper, she could just be referring to herself. Rumor has it she was in love with him at one time and he, ultimately, was not in love with her.

Eventually Mr. London does exactly what I know he'll do: he walks out the door. He does this in the classroom when he gets upset and doesn't want people to see him upset. He knows he has an anger management problem and his way of controlling it is to leave. When he exits the classroom we all sit still and count to 120 aloud in unison because we know that he is counting two minutes before he comes back in. Two minutes must be the amount of time he was taught was both advisable and permissible to leave and calm down before reentering a room.

Now that Mr. London has left the teacher's lounge, I know I have two minutes alone. I hadn't planned on doing what I do. From my shorts pocket, I remove the three birth control pills I smuggled from sex ed class and crumble them in the palm of my left hand. Then I stand and approach the coffeepot and release the powder. I take a dirty spoon from the sink and stir the coffee. There's no trace of the pills. I sit back down and think that already it smells a little less like testosterone. I imagine it smells more like the gym where my mother does aerobics with all her new friends. Mr. London returns to the lounge in exactly 120 seconds. I'm sitting where he left me.

"I have decided that you are entitled to your opinion about *Franny and Zooey*," he says, and takes a sip of his coffee.

"Thank you," I say, and stand.

7

Friday is a half day at school, thank god. I'm still getting the silent treatment from all my classmates. That afternoon my parents have to go to a cocktail reception and auction at my father's art gallery. They've asked Petra, the daughter of my mom's longtime supervisor at the hospital, to babysit. I don't need a babysitter but given the events of the week and the fact that they will be out late at a post-auction dinner, they ask her to come keep me and Svea company. Petra is twenty and has wild pitch-black hair that she usually positions on top of her head with chopsticks. I once complimented her hairstyle and now she gives me chopsticks every year for my birthday. I have a pile of chopsticks on a shelf of my closet, next to the small safe where I keep money I've earned from babysitting.

My father has been getting ready for the auction all week. He's going to be the auctioneer and he goes through a series of tongue twisters to prepare. It's been a few months since the last auction and he says his tongue is "rusty." He sits alone in the study with a gavel and rattles through numbers and then says, "going once, going twice." Regardless of where I am in the house, I can hear the gavel hitting the table and my father's voice yelling "Sold!"

Friday is officially hot—San Francisco's summer has finally arrived in the fall. My mother gets off early from work and bikes home and washes and styles her hair and paints her nails. She dresses in all white and I have to admit she looks glamorous, and my father says so, too. "Wow," he says when she comes downstairs. He stands at a distance, appraising her like art.

Petra arrives at the back door at 2:30 with pink chopsticks in her hair. She's wearing shorts and a T-shirt that says "You Wish." I'm glad Petra is seeing my mother dressed up. She usually sees her in her nurse's scrubs or her exercise attire. My parents give her instructions on what to feed us (pasta) and when they'll be home (after eleven) and then they are gone— off to the art gallery to make sure everything is in order for the evening ahead. My father comes back into the house because he's forgotten his gavel. "Can't leave without this," he says, and Petra smiles at him in return. There's something about the way Petra smiles at him that always makes my chest tighten like I'm in an elevator that's gotten stuck.

"Didn't my mom look sexy?" I say.

"Hmm," Petra says, and I immediately regret asking. Five seconds pass, then fifteen. "She looked very pretty, but I wouldn't call her sexy."

"What's the difference?" I say.

"Well, her beauty is not a sexual one," Petra says, and by the way she says it I can tell that Petra thinks of herself as a sexual beauty.

I head into the front room to escape. Every room in our house has a name—front room, library, foyer, lower level. (Never call it the basement.) From the front windows of our house I can see the traffic snaking to the beach. It's not even 3, but it appears everyone's left work early to enjoy the rare heat. "We should go!" Petra says. She's come up behind me. She tells me some classmates from UC Berkeley—she calls it "Cal"— will be at the beach and asks if we want to invite any friends. Svea wants to invite her dour friend.

"Isn't there anyone you want to invite?" Petra asks.

"No," I say casually. "I'm tired of my friends."

She stares at me with her petrifying eyes.

She knows. My parents must have told her about my week, about the fact that no one's talking to me at school. The teachers must have called them.

The mom of the dour friend drops her off in her convertible in a matter of minutes. Her mother is single and always happy, and it occurs to me, is made even happier by the prospect of dropping off her unsmiling daughter. Maybe it means she can go on a date. "Good-bye," she calls to us from the foot of the stairs. She waves a big theatrical wave, as though she's on a cruise ship leaving shore.

I put on shorts and an Esprit T-shirt—not normal beach attire. Normal beach attire where we live is a parka. "Don't you want to put on a swimsuit?" Petra asks me, Svea, and the dour friend. No, we tell her, we don't want to put on swimsuits. "Well, I've got mine on underneath," Petra says. I'm slightly relieved by this fact because it means that she'll likely take off her "You Wish" T-shirt once we get to the beach. I can only imagine the comments it's going to inspire.

But when we arrive at the beach and Petra takes off her T-shirt and shorts, I wish she'd put her shorts back on. Her pubic hair is black and bushy and extends beyond the elastic of her bikini bottom and onto her thighs for at least two inches.

Petra spots her friends from college and she hugs them and then they start playing Frisbee. She's up and running along the beach, in front of the sunbathers, her pubes on full display and shining in the sunlight. I can't look. I turn away and that's when I spot Maria Fabiola. She's on the cliffs, climbing—I know her climbing style. It's swift and nimble. There's another figure lumbering behind her and I can't make out who it is at first. Then I see that it's Lotta, the new girl from Holland. Lotta invited me to her house tomorrow night for a birthday sleepover party, but she handed me the invitation last week before everything else happened so all bets are off. She's five foot seven and is wearing bright red shorts and an orange T-shirt. She started at Spragg this year and so far I've only seen her in a uniform. In her beach clothes she looks much more Dutch. She's trailing behind Maria Fabiola by about twenty feet. She's from a flat country and is no match for this terrain, and I can imagine Maria Fabiola's exasperation with her. Maybe Maria Fabiola will miss me, I think.

There are over a hundred people on the beach today, when usually there are three. On a typical day there's a couple writing their names in the sand and surrounding their writing with a heart. And a lone man or woman staring at the sea, contemplating the future or past. But on this late afternoon everyone's eyes are on other people's bodies. Men in tight swim-suits and girls in white bikinis with the dark of their nipples showing through. Weaving among them all is Petra, theatrically catching a Frisbee and hiding it behind her back. She wants someone to tackle her for it. Specifically, she wants one of her male friends with long hair and a stocky torso to fall on top of her.

On the towel beside me, Svea and her dour friend are playing a game of cards. They're both wearing sweat suits, which I choose to view as a rebuke to Petra, and silently applaud them for their choice in attire. I close my eyes and sink into the sand. A cloud moves and the sun takes aim at my skin.

I sleep a light sleep for ten minutes, maybe fifteen. When I open my eyes I feel a body near me. It's Keith, from Sea View Terrace. Even though he's sitting, he's still tall, burying his feet in the sand.

"Hey," I say.

"Hey," he says, his eyes blue as globes. "You're awake."

I sit up. Petra isn't in sight and Svea and her dour friend are walking up the concrete stairs—probably going to the restrooms that smell like dirty fish tanks.

"What are you doing?" I ask. My voice sounds sleepy, seductive. I don't clear my throat.

"I just came down here to check it out. See what the beach would look like on an actual beach day." He's wearing shorts and a white surf T-shirt that's been worn and washed enough that it's thin and, I imagine, soft.

"Same," I say.

I look at his feet, buried in sand to the ankles. I know why he's done that. I slowly sweep sand from his toes. I look up at him to make sure what I'm doing is okay. His long, oval face looks pained but he nods. I continue running my fingers over the sand, gently, as though I'm excavating, searching for delicate treasure.

I've never seen his webbed feet before. I've only heard about them. "Spiderman," his not-close friends call him. His best friends know he's too sensitive for that. His feet are wide and not webbed like a duck's the way I thought they would be. Instead, the toes are attached halfway down, and then each toe is independent right near where his toenails start. I don't know what possesses me, but I bend over and my lips graze the knuckles of his toes in one slow stretch from second toe to little toe. I get sand in my mouth but don't spit it out.

I look up at him and I think I see a tear in the corner of one of his blue eyes.

"It's bright out," he says.

"Yeah," I say so he's not embarrassed. "I forgot to bring my Ray-Bans."

"Want to go for a walk?" he says.

I stand and he turns to the left, but that's where I last saw Maria Fabiola and Lotta, so I gesture to the right. "Let's go this way," I say.

We run into Petra as we stroll. Or rather, she runs into us. "Hey. I'm Petra," she says to Keith.

"Okay," he says. He must assume she's an overly friendly stranger.

"She's a family friend," I explain. "She's babysitting my sister."

"Oh," he says. "I'm Keith."

I think I see him glance down at her pubic hair, and I get embarrassed for her. "Where you going?" she says to me.

"We'll be back in five minutes," I say.

"Okay," she says and lifts her chin up, as though to say *I'm cool. I know better than to say, "Have fun."*

Keith and I walk to the cliffs. Someone's spray-painted "ABC" on a large rock. That's the tag of one of the local gangs of teenagers. "ABC" stands for "American Born Chinese." The other tag you see around the neighborhood is "CBS," which stands for "Can't Be Stopped," which is a group of skateboarders. To an outsider, it might seem that the news teams are competing. I show Keith how to time the waves. Then I yell "run" and we make our way to the other side of the promontory before a wave crashes against the rock. The enormous splash looks like something that would be captured in a bad oil painting. We stand on the other side of the promontory not talking, not touching, just breathing loudly in unison. After our exhalations have quieted, I show Keith how to run back.

When we're on the main beach again we see Petra in the distance and Keith says he's going to walk home. "Okay," I say. "See ya."

"See ya," he says.

I return to the towel where I was sleeping and see that someone's written "Slut" in the sand next to it. I look around to see who could have written it. I think about using my hand to erase it, but then don't. Now I have a tag, too.

8

The next day Lotta calls me and disinvites me to her birthday party. "The problem is I'm new and trying to make friends and no one will come if you come."

"I get it," I say. I do.

I end up going to an engagement party with my parents that night while my sister goes to a sleepover. The party is for the eldest son of our Gold Rush neighbors. There are often work parties at the house that we're not invited to because they're for bankers. But tonight's celebration is personal, neighborly. The eldest son, Wes, is engaged and tonight's a party for him and his soon-to-be bride. I don't know Wes that well—he left home for Dartmouth five years ago, and after graduating, he moved to Boston.

We enter the house through the front door, which is a first—I'm accustomed to leaping through the window. The entranceway is dim: the windows are tinted and curtained and the floors are dark. My house is light, with mirrors everywhere. This is the result of a design trick my parents adopted when they were younger and broke and wanted their living spaces to appear larger than they were. Now that they live in a big house, they still haven't abandoned the mirrors.

Mr. Finance and his wife greet us. She's thin and wearing a large diamond necklace that doesn't rest flat and makes me notice how much her clavicle juts out. Her dress is emerald green and her blond hair is pulled back to the nape of her neck. Standing behind the host couple is their elderly Irish maid, wearing a uniform. She's holding a silver tray with glasses of champagne. I have only seen the maid from a distance, when she hangs hand-washed items outside a window that faces our house. Apparently, no one has told her this is not a neighborhood where you hang your laundry outside windows to dry.

My parents' faces look suddenly strained, and I know the forced smiles and tightness around the eyes has to do with me. I turn and see Maria Fabiola's parents. Their arms are linked as though they're the bride and groom.

"Where's Maria Fabiola tonight?" my father asks her dapperly dressed father as we stand together in an awkward pentagram.

"She's at a sleepover at a new girl's house. Dutch family."

"Have you met her?" my father asks me.

"She's in my class."

My mother makes small talk with Maria Fabiola's mom about Halloween and how many bags of candy they're going to purchase this year. Halloween is a big deal in Sea Cliff. Residents go crazy giving out dollar bills or King Size Hershey's bars, and as a result each house gets hundreds of trick-or-treaters before 7 p.m. Kids from other parts of the city are dropped off in Sea Cliff by their parents because they know they'll take home better loot here than anywhere else.

Another couple who just moved to the neighborhood joins the conversation. "I hear they're going to try to clamp down on outsiders coming in," says the woman, who has an accent I can't place.

"They really should," says her husband. "It's not right for us to be spending all that money on kids that don't live here."

I excuse myself to use the restroom.

The bathroom is large with a wooden sculpture of a boy peeing. When I wash my hands I use a small towel that I understand I'm supposed to toss into a special bin. Outside the bathroom door I hear someone ask, "Are you waiting in line?" Then I hear the response: "No, I'm just escaping talking to someone I don't want to talk to. You know how it is." I recognize the voice—it's Maria Fabiola's mother. I use another towel just because I can and toss it in the bin as well. Then I take a towel and without even using it, discard it in the bin.

When I exit the bathroom I offer Maria Fabiola's mother a fake smile. I scan the room for my parents—I don't want to go back to them. I spot an abandoned glass of champagne on a small table. I stealthily pick it up, down it, and then wander into the part of the house I know best: the TV room. I think I might find the younger brother there watching TV with his friends and I can show them how grown up I look in my black taffeta dress. I walk into the TV room and the screen is dark, most of the lights in the room are off. I look through the window to see what my house looks like from here. It looks like a regular house, I think. On my bedroom window I see a faded sticker alerting firemen that, in the event of a fire, there's a child living in that bedroom. The sticker was placed there years ago and I'd forgotten about it. Now I vow to remove it.

"Aren't you the neighbor girl?" a voice asks. I turn. It's Wes, the older brother, the groom-to-be. He's sitting by himself in the dark.

I nod and then realize he probably can't see me very well so I say, "Yeah."

We are both silent as we listen to the sounds of the party swell in the other part of the house.

"Aren't you supposed to be out there?" I ask. "I mean, isn't the party for you?"

"Well, in theory it's for me, but it's really for my parents."

I nod again. He's blond and wearing a tuxedo. He looks like a groom in a movie, which makes him appear more handsome than he is. More handsome than his younger brother.

"My head hurts so I came in here," he says.

I know he was in a major hockey accident at Dartmouth. He came home to recuperate for a while. The maid would hang his clothes outside the laundry-room window. One day his clothes were no longer there and I knew he was better, and had gone back to New Hampshire.

"Does it hurt?" I ask.

"Just when I'm stressed."

"Why are you stressed now?"

"Because I'm getting married," he says.

His speech is slurred and I wonder if this is the result of the accident or alcohol. I continue standing in front of the turned-off TV and I shift from one foot to another. Tonight I'm wearing black shoes with short heels. I'm not used to them but don't want to take them off because that would show I'm not used to them.

"Have you ever heard of that experiment they do with frogs?" he asks.

"Which one?" I say, and tap my fingers on my chin, as though I'm running through all the experiments I've studied involving frogs.

"The one where they put a frog in boiling water?"

"I think so," I lie.

"They've done studies where if they put a frog in boiling water, it jumps out right away."

"That makes sense," I say.

"Well, they've also done studies where if they put a frog in, let's say, medium-temperature water, and then slowly keep turning up the heat until it's boiling, the frog won't jump out."

"It won't?"

"No, it won't. And you know what happens to the frog?"

"What?"

"It dies," he says. "This is a scientific fact."

He leans back on the leather couch and takes a sip of his drink. I think about what he's said. I assume it's a metaphor for marriage.

"So, you're the frog," I finally say.

"Ribbit," he says.

I'm not sure if I should leave so I stand there in front of the large, blank television screen, and he watches me as if I'm the show.

"Have you ever given someone a lap dance?" he asks.

"I don't think so," I say.

"You don't think so," he says and laughs. The champagne rises up, prickling my throat, and then settles back down.

"Come here," he says, his voice quiet and smooth.

The room is so dim that I suddenly feel tired. As I approach him, he signals to me to turn around and I do. I sit on his lap so we're both facing the same direction. The taffeta skirt of my dress rises. He places his hands on my hips and moves them in a figure-eight pattern. I stare straight ahead at the dark screen of the TV. I can make out the image of a young girl writhing around and the head of a young man thrown back. Maybe his accident really did hurt his head, I think, as he moans. Soon there's a rush of heat, followed by wetness.

"Oh," he moans. He holds me to him so my spine is pressed to his front. It's uncomfortable and I don't know how long I'm obliged to sit like that. I count to ten and then I stand and don't turn around. I want to give him privacy.

I know I'll see his underwear hanging outside the laundry-room window the next morning. *The poor maid* is all I can think as I straighten my dress out so it doesn't poof. She's over eighty and tomorrow she'll be cleaning semen off Wes's underpants.

9

October arrives but the palm trees don't change color. China Beach is empty except for the fishermen who wait patiently on the cliffs in the early morning. Sometimes they wade out into the water to fish, despite the signs that appear at the entrance to the beach announcing: "People have drowned while swimming or wading." The warning is in English, Chinese, Russian, and Spanish.

Fall gives the flashers who like to stroll by Spragg an excuse to wear trench coats. The upper school classrooms have large windows that look out onto the public golf course that runs adjacent to the back of the campus. It's not uncommon for us to glance outside the window when distracted or bored and spot a man standing with his trench coat open, exposing himself. "Just pretend you don't see him and keep your focus on me," Ms. Livesey tells us whenever a flasher shows up. My father says I should point at the flashers and laugh. These are two very different approaches. Everything I'm told by one adult contradicts something I'm told by another.

On the evening of October 30 my parents realize I don't have a costume. I tell them it's okay and I ask my mother if I can borrow a scarf. Then I weave one end of the scarf through the spokes of an old bike wheel. I wrap the other end of it around my neck and carry the wheel in my hands.

"Who are you?" Svea asks.

"Isadora Duncan," I tell her.

"Who's that?"

"She was a dancer who died of strangulation when the wind blew her scarf out of the car and the scarf got stuck in the wheel."

"That's terrible," Svea says.

I shrug. "Fashion can be dangerous."

On Halloween Maria Fabiola, Julia, Faith, and Lotta come to school dressed like the Go-Go's on the cover of "Beauty and the Beat." They're dressed in white bathrobes (on the album cover, the Go-Go's wear towels, tucked precariously over their breasts, but this was probably deemed too risqué by my friends' parents). To their faces they've applied masks of a white substance that has hardened and cracked on their cheeks. Their teeth look yellow in comparison. The group outfit was my idea; I shared it with them in September, a century ago. Lotta, the Dutch girl, didn't know who the Go-Go's were before she came to America. There are five members of the band, but on Halloween at Spragg there are only four.

At school the teachers vote and give me the Best Costume award, which is an awful decision. I know they choose me as the winner because they can see I've been ostracized, that I have no one to talk to. Don't they know that awarding me and my costume that I started making at 8:15 the previous evening is more humiliating?

On Halloween night I take Svea and her dour friend trick-or-treating. Then we give out candy at our house until the big black cauldron is empty.

"We're all out of candy," I yell to my parents, who are in the kitchen.

"We can't let them know we're home or they'll egg the house," my dad yells.

"Turn off the lights," my mom commands.

We enter a state of high alert. We blow out all the candles inside the jack-o'-lanterns that line the front steps to our house. Then, as a precautionary measure, we carry the carved pumpkins inside. The light switches are turned off so that it appears no one's home. Sitting near the windows is deemed too risky so we huddle on the carpet on the floor of the foyer. "I feel like Anne Frank hiding from the Nazis," my sister's dour friend says.

Even in the dimness I see something I've never seen on her face before—a smile.

10

My mother is in a Swedish sewing group. That is, it started off as a sewing group called the Stitch 'N' Bitch but it's been a year or so since anyone's brought their dress patterns or quilt squares to the monthly meetings. Last winter my mom started calling it the Bitch 'N' Bitch because she wanted to chide the members about their constant complaining and cajole them into focusing on sewing. Her ploy backfired—the group loved the phrase so much that they adopted it as their official name. They left their sewing baskets at home and started complaining even more.

Tonight it's my mother's turn to host the monthly Bitch 'N' Bitch meeting. It's a special night: the TV episode filmed at Joseph & Joseph is airing this evening. I leave notes in Maria Fabiola's, Julia's, and

Faith's lockers making sure they know the show starts at 7. My hope is that it reminds them of how close we used to be.

From the way my mom torpedoes through the door that afternoon I can tell she spent her bike ride home from the hospital making a mental list of all she needs to get done. She asks Svea to help her in the kitchen with the meatballs and the lutefisk. For reasons I don't fully understand, I'm not trusted in the kitchen—it's my mother and Svea's terrain.

"How can I help?" I ask, trying to secure an invitation into the quiet camaraderie of meal preparation.

"Hmm . . . maybe you can make a welcome sign for the guests," my mom says. "You can hang it on the front door."

"But some of your friends come through the back door," I say. I want to be included, not make a sign.

"Then you should put a sign on the back door telling them to go around to the front door," Svea suggests.

"Good idea," my mom says.

I take sheets of paper and colored pencils from the art supply drawer and make two signs, using an orange pen and my finest approximation of calligraphy. One sign says: "Welcome Bitchers!" The other says: "Bitchers! You came to the wrong door. Bitch yourself around to the front."

My father comes home from work as I'm taping the sign up to the back door.

"That will show them," he says.

"Why do you think they complain so much?" I say. "I mean, it seems the main thing they complain about is America. Sometimes, I want to yell, 'Go back to Sweden!'"

"How do you think I feel?" my dad says. "They use 'American' as a negative."

"They tell me I don't look Swedish because of my dark eyes," I say. "They mean it as an insult."

Then we sigh almost in unison because the truth is we kind of love the Bitchers. They're good friends to my mom.

It's a brisk November evening. At 6 p.m., when the doorbell rings, my family falls into their Bitch 'N' Bitch party-hosting positions. My mother opens the door for her guests, my father offers each of them a drink, and Svea walks around with a tray of meatballs that have been stabbed with toothpicks bearing the Swedish flag. Somewhere between the opening of the door and the offering of meatballs, it's my job to collect the coats and hang them in the hall closet.

There are a dozen members of the Bitch 'N' Bitch; many of them have the same name, so each woman has been given an adjective. There's Tall Mia, Short Mia,

Fat Ulla, Thin Ulla (whose California license plates say "Uuulala"), Loud Lisa, and Quiet Lisa. They really call themselves by these names. Things got complicated when Fat Ulla did a juice fast and dropped a couple dress sizes, and Thin Ulla gained weight during menopause, but no one bothered to change their monikers—not even Fat and Thin Ulla themselves. My mother is the only Greta.

As a group, they are blond and punctual. My arms are promptly loaded up with similar lightweight wool coats, each smelling crisp, like business envelopes that have just been sealed. Tall Mia is the last to arrive, and her coat stands out in the closet—it's the only pink one. She once got her colors done and was told summer was her most complementary palette. She promptly discarded any article of clothing that wasn't pink or orange. Her nail polish is usually one of these two colors, as is her lipstick. Tonight Tall Mia is wearing burnt orange pants and a burnt orange blouse so that the overall effect is that of a large autumnal leaf that's fallen from a tree. She sits on the backless imitation Louis XIV couch, which is like a daybed, with cylindrical ivory pillows.

I approach her and sit near her because I can usually count on Tall Mia to prop me up. She's the one who tells me that my style is impeccable and that I resemble

Sonja Henie, the Norwegian figure skater. She started making the Sonja Henie remark one day when she was at our house and I was coming back from an ice-skating party for Julia's birthday. So I think her praise has more to do with the fact that she once saw me in ice-skating apparel than my appearance. But she is different this evening, and I am shallow, I think, to come to her wanting reinforcement.

"You can't count on men," Tall Mia says. "Those boys? The fancy boys at dancing school? You should forget about them. Believe me. Steve is fancy and he has been nothing but bad news."

Steve is the married man she's been dating. He's been the subject of many Bitch 'N' Bitch conversations. None of the Bitchers think Tall Mia should be dating a married man. They don't seem to object on moral grounds—their collective reservation has more to do with the nuisance of it all. They treat her relationship with Steve the same way they would treat the idea of getting a puppy. Why would you get a new puppy when you'd spend weeks training it and cleaning up after it? Why date a married man when that means you have to deal with a wife? These women are very practical.

"I'm going to jump," Tall Mia informs me.

I look at her, not knowing what she means. Then I follow her gaze to the Golden Gate Bridge.

"You'll probably hurt yourself," I say. It's the first thought that comes to mind.

"Then Steve will know the pain he's caused me."

I look around the room and quickly understand why I'm sitting alone with Tall Mia. The Bitchers warned Tall Mia, they expressed their distaste for her affair, and now she is my problem. Aside from feeling a little out of my depth, I don't mind. I know most thirteen-year-olds are sheltered from this kind of conversation, so I'm proud to be privy to it. I rest my head on an ivory bolster and listen to Tall Mia talk about Steve and how she's going to kill herself as though it's a good-night story. At some point she switches from speaking in English to Swinglish, and then she makes the transition from Swinglish to pure Swedish. She's speaking quickly and intently and I'm having trouble grasping exactly what she's saying. But I listen to her words and see her mouth moving and I know that she's telling me something terrible and suicidal and probably not at all suitable.

"Okay," my mom says, and claps her hands together loudly. "Let's move into the study to watch the show!"

We all gather in the study—Svea, my parents, and I sit on the rug to make room for all the Bitchers. We turn the TV on five minutes before 7 because we don't want to miss the establishing shot.

Someone asks me for water and I ignore them. Then the show starts and we get a quick glimpse of Joseph & Joseph's exterior. Then the next scene shows the interior of the gallery. "What happened to the establishing shot?" I say.

"Shh," say some of the Bitchers, loudly.

"I'm sure they'll use that shot later," my dad says.

But we watch the whole episode and toward the end of it, it becomes evident that Maria Fabiola, Julia, Faith, Svea, and I have been cut. I look at Svea and she shrugs. She doesn't know how important it was to me to be in the show. She doesn't know how I was counting on my friends seeing it, and things going back to normal.

The final credits roll and the Bitchers applaud. I excuse myself, claiming exhaustion, and say I have to study for a big test. I make a point of hugging Tall Mia. The hug is awkward, as she's still seated, but the elliptical embrace allows me the chance to whisper in her ear: "Don't take the bridge on the way home."

"Why would I?" she says, not whispering. "I live in the other direction."

Upstairs in my room, I can hear the women laughing and the occasional clattering of silverware—they've moved into the dining room for lutefisk. I hear collective gasps and wonder what story is being told and about whom.

I think of other TV shows and movies and how every movie star must be upset about a scene that was cut. I recently saw *Out of Africa*—my mom took me to the theater because she wanted to see the film and I had no plans. Since then I've thought a lot about the scene with Robert Redford washing Meryl Streep's hair. Now *that*, I thought, is love. And Meryl Streep's skin looked incredible.

I get up and check my complexion in the bathroom mirror. Four zits, not terrible. Not as bad as some of the girls in my class. Poor Angie. I reapply Clearasil and go back in my room and do twenty sit-ups. Then I lay in bed listening to the explosions of laughter, followed by the rearranging of chairs, the trickling of voices, and the closing of the front door. My room is directly above the kitchen and I hear my mother tidying up after the party. I picture her pulling on the gloves she uses when cleaning dishes. This is the same sink where she used to wash my hair. She'd place towels on the kitchen counter and I'd rest on top of them, with my head extending out to the faucet, and she'd shampoo my hair and talk about her day. Now I listen to her turn on the water—I find the sound comforting. I spread out my hair on the pillow like Medusa, like Meryl Streep, and imagine it's my hair my mother's washing in the sink, the way she did when I was young.

11

In Swedish culture December 13 is a holiday. A ritual. The oldest girl in the house acts out the part of Santa Lucia, dressed in white and wearing a crown of lighted candles, waking her family with singing and saffron buns.

My radio alarm clock goes off early, and after staying in bed to listen to the end of a Police song, I get up. I slip on the white, ironed nightgown that my mother has hung from the doorknob to my room. She's done this—the ironing and the hanging—while I was sleeping.

Quietly, I walk downstairs to the kitchen and remove several saffron buns from a cookie tin and place them on a silver tray. I find matches in a drawer and contemplate the crown of candles. This is the hardest part—placing the crown of candles on my head and walking up the stairs. It requires balance, and when the wax drips down onto my scalp, it burns. I decide to carry everything up to the second floor. Then I light the candles and secure the crown on my head. I pick up the tray of saffron buns and walk into my parents' room. Their door has conveniently been left wide open for this annual ritual. I start to sing the Santa Lucia song about how dark the night is, and my parents quickly sit up in bed. I can tell they've already been awake, waiting. I finish the first verse of the song and place the tray on a side table.

Sock-footed, I step into Svea's room. She's a heavy sleeper and hard to rouse. I'm singing loudly and the candle wax is starting to drip onto my head. Finally, I give up singing Swedish. "Wake up!" I yell. Svea sits up and I squat down, and she knows to help me blow out the candles. "Use your hands," I say, and she cups each candle before she blows.

Still, I find myself picking wax out of my hair on the way to school.

I have stopped walking by Julia's and Faith's houses—instead I take a different route, with Svea and her dour friend, who is dourer today because we are late. The Santa Lucia ritual has set us back several minutes. We walk past the castle, past the house that once belonged to Carter the Great, past the pink house that belongs to the woman who went to Palm Springs for the weekend and impulsively got a tummy tuck. "Who gets a tummy tuck on a whim?" I've heard other women comment, as though it was the last-minute nature of her procedure that was most shocking. In the distance, foghorns sound, and near us, leaf blowers make their loud leaf-blowing sound. The streets are empty as usual. But at the entrance to the school, there's a commotion, and causing the commotion are three police cars.

The headmaster's secretary is standing stiffly outside the front office. She never stands outside the office. When she sees me approaching, her body relaxes, and then tightens again. She asks if she can speak to me for a minute.

I go inside the office. She waits for the door to close. "Maria Fabiola is missing," she tells me. "She disappeared yesterday when walking home from school. The detectives want to talk to you."

12

The meeting with Mr. Makepeace and the detectives takes place in a conference room at the back of the office. Probably because there's more room. There are three detectives waiting to talk with me—a man with tight pants, a man with loose pants, and—surprise!—a woman. She has dyed blond hair pulled severely into a ponytail, and very thin lips. Her eyes are upon me the moment I pass through the conference room door.

"I'm Detective Anderson," she says. "And you're Eulabee."

I agree that that is my name.

"That's a beautiful name," she says. "Where is it from?"

It's evident they've decided that she's going to be kind to me, that she's going to sweet-talk me so I will give her answers.

"It's from a painting," I say. "My dad liked a painting of a woman named Eulabee Dix."

"Interesting," she says, showing no interest. She is already looking down at her clipboard, thinking of her next question. "Do you know why we called you in here today?" she asks.

I look at Mr. Makepeace, who nods at me. His blue bow tie bounces up and down.

"Because he told you to call me in," I say, nodding back at the headmaster.

"And why do you think he did that?" Detective Anderson says.

"Because I used to be best friends with Maria Fabiola."

"Used to be?" she says. Now she does seem genuinely interested. She puts her pen down, to show that we are about to have a serious conversation. "Why used to? What happened, my dear?"

The *dear* sounds so forced coming out of her mouth that I want to laugh.

"We had a falling out."

"About what?"

I don't say anything.

"Was it about a boy?" she says in a tone that's meant to convey *we can all relate to that*.

"No," I say.

"Oh," she says, clearly disappointed that she has not tapped in to the root problem with her first guess. She looks at the other detectives.

"You were friends a couple months ago."

"Things change," I tell her.

"Don't I know it," she says. "Six months ago I was married!" She lets out a laugh that I think is supposed to sound jovial but instead sounds more like a scream.

Mr. Makepeace looks at me, as though he, too, is curious about my falling out with Maria Fabiola. Or maybe he's just upset because he wants a cigar and this conference room has a "No Smoking" sign that was posted specifically to target him. No one else in the administration smokes.

"You used to walk to school together, didn't you?" the detective with the tight pants asks.

"Yes, but then we had a . . . difference of opinion about what happened that morning." I've never used the phrase "difference of opinion" before and I like how it sounds.

"What was the difference?" the detective with the loose pants asks.

"She said there was an incident on the way to school, and I maintained that the incident was a fabrication," I say. Everyone is looking at me as though wondering where I got my vocabulary from. Then they look at Mr. Makepeace, who shrugs, unsurprised, as if to suggest, *What else did you expect from the girls at our fine institution?*

"So you didn't walk home with Maria Fabiola yesterday," Detective Anderson says.

"No," I say.

"Do you know what route she would have taken?"

"I can guess," I say. "We used to walk home together. She probably walked toward the ocean and then followed El Camino del Mar to her house."

"Do you think she took a detour? That she walked by the cliffs?" the third detective asks.

"I don't know," I say. "I wasn't with her."

"Does she have a boyfriend?" Detective Anderson asks. It must have been established ahead of time that she would be asking me all the questions that had to do with boys or relationships.

"I don't know," I say again.

Detective Anderson looks down and balances her forehead on the thumb and forefinger of her right hand, as though she's tired. Her ponytail flops to the side the way a horse's tail moves when the horse is about to urinate. When she straightens up her head, her eyes are full of fire and desperation. "You realize that your best friend has gone missing, don't you?"

I want to remind her that Maria Fabiola is no longer my best friend, but I sense this correction will further enrage the detective.

"Yes," I say.

"And you're not concerned?"

"I am concerned," I say. What I don't say is that I'm more concerned about how easily I seem to upset people recently—first Mr. London, now her. My capacity to ignite fury seems to know no gender boundaries.

"Can I ask a question?" the detective with tight pants says.

"Didn't you just do that by asking?" Detective Anderson retorts.

The detective clears his throat. They are tired of each other already. Either that, I think, or they're going to go fuck after this. I have many different and somewhat contradictory ideas of how adult seduction works.

"Do you know of any reason why Maria Fabiola might have . . . run away? You mentioned you had a falling out. Has she been . . . left out of things in the last months? Has she had friends?"

"She's had plenty of friends," I say. "I'm the one who's been ostracized."

The three officers stare at me. Then all at once, they turn to their notebooks and scribble. The officer with the loose pants peers over at Detective Anderson's notebook. "It's T-R-A-C-I-Z," she says. Then she turns to me.

"Has anyone ever approached you and Maria Fabiola in a way that you thought was . . . inappropriate?" Detective Anderson says.

I think of the flashers in the park, of the man in line at Walgreens who saw me with a Kinks album under my arm. I was coming from a record store in the Haight and he offered to take me to coffee and talk about the Kinks. "I don't drink coffee yet," I told the man at Walgreens.

"I don't really know what you mean by that," I say to the detective.

"Have they ever made you feel uncomfortable?"

"Everyone makes me feel uncomfortable," I say. "I feel uncomfortable right now."

The men in the room roll back on the wheels of their chairs, retreating. Detective Anderson is now going to be the only one asking questions.

"Your friend is missing," she says. "Her family is, well, her family is freaking out. They are crying and screaming. Can you imagine how your family would feel if you were missing?"

I nod, unable to picture it. My mother doesn't cry.

"And Maria Fabiola is probably scared to death, too, wherever she is. You might be able to help us, to help her. I understand you two aren't close anymore, but in the scheme of things, having a falling out for a couple months isn't a big deal. It might feel like that now, but honey, when you're older those three months will feel like a quick blip." She snaps when she says the word "blip."

I stare at her.

"Is there any information you have about any men, or anybody in general that you think might have had an interest that went beyond normal in Maria Fabiola?"

"An interest beyond normal," I repeat.

"Yes, anyone who wanted her to himself, for example." She pauses and adds: "Or herself."

I think of Faith's father. I think of the boys of Sea View Terrace. I think of myself. Everyone always wants more of Maria Fabiola to themselves. There is something about how she focuses on you with those ethereal eyes. Even when you aren't looking directly at her—especially when you aren't looking directly at her—you can see that she's staring at you, her eyes unblinking.

A minute goes by, maybe two. I can't mention the boys of Sea Cliff, that wouldn't be fair. If anything, we have more of an interest in the boys of Sea Cliff than they have in us. But I do feel the pressure to provide an answer.

"Is there anyone you encounter on your walks to and from school on a regular basis?" Detective Tight Pants asks.

"There are a couple gardeners who harass us," I say.

"Who?" the detectives ask in unison. They all lean in, like an a cappella group singing a high note.

"Well, there are a few. I don't know their names. They have trucks and they all wear white under-shirts as their T-shirts. They usually comment on our appearance."

"What do they say about your appearance?" Detective Anderson asks with slow deliberate words. She's trying so hard to be calm.

"They noticed when we started wearing bras. These white blouses don't help."

I sense that everyone in the room is sitting up taller. It's like a fishing line going suddenly taut.

"What do you mean they noticed? How did they notice?"

"They comment. They chase after us."

What I don't say is that they chase us away some-times when we're bothering them. Sometimes when we're bored on the streets of Sea Cliff, when the neighborhood boys seem to be gone, in some place in the city we can't find or get to, we approach the gardeners and try to talk with them. That's when they chase us away.

The detectives seem happy with my response.

"Well, we have a lead," Tight Pants says. Detective Anderson slides me her business card. "Call me if anything else occurs to you." I take the card and don't know what to do with it. I don't think I've ever held a business card before. I lift up my skirt and the male detectives look away. They don't know we wear gym shorts under our uniforms. I place the card in a pocket of my shorts.

I enter science midway through class. There's a drawing of a penis being projected onto the screen, its parts labeled.

At recess, rumors swirl. We see the vans of news stations surrounding our campus. We're ushered back inside the classrooms, which makes us more stir-crazy. When the air-raid siren goes off at noon we all scream. It's hard to distinguish between the siren and our screams, but we keep going even after the siren has ceased. We know it's a practice drill but things are tense. Even the teachers seem at a loss about what do without Maria Fabiola at school. The desks she normally occupies in each classroom seem extraordinarily shiny.

By the time school lets out, all the students are acting frenzied. The news trucks are still surrounding our school. There are more of them now. NBC. ABC. KPIX. Well-coiffed anchorwomen in suits and pearls stand beyond the school gates, their backs to us, commenting. I'm sure they're using the words "private," "elite," "wealthy" as often as they can. Every parent has been called and asked to pick up their daughter after school. None of the mothers work except for my mom, so I call her at the hospital. I know her work phone number by heart because it's the punch line of a story. My mother entertained our guests at a dinner party one night by telling them about the looks she gets when she's at work and leaves a message on a fellow Swede's answering machine. She'll ask them to call her back and then give them the phone number—666–7777—which in Swedish sounds like *Sex! Sex! Sex! Who? Who? Who? Who?*

I dial the number now.

"She's in the OR," Mrs. Markson says. Mrs. Markson is my mother's supervisor and Petra's mom. She asks if she can take a message. "No," I tell her. She congratulates me on winning third place in the hospital contest for kids. I designed a new nurses' locker room. Svea won the contest and received $400. I got a subscription to a teen magazine I don't read.

After school, the parents line up in the horseshoe-shaped driveway by the field. The pick-up process is slow and made slower by the fact that every mother gets out of the car to talk to other mothers about Maria Fabiola's disappearance. The caravan looks like an ad for Volvo. I see the dour friend's mom picking up her daughter and my sister. The mom now waves as though she's just returned from a cruise. *Hello! I missed you! I have presents!*

I sneak out the back gate while the parents line up at the front one. I start walking. I don't go into my house, but instead grab my bike from the garage and pedal quickly to where I suspect Maria Fabiola is hiding.

13

I stop my bike across the street from the Olenska School of Ballet, in front of the comic-book store. The studio's floor-to-ceiling curtains are closed. I move my gaze up to the apartment above the studio, where Madame Sonya lives. She often complains of hot flashes that didn't cease even after she completed menopause, so she likes to keep the windows cracked. But now the windows are shut—a good indicator she isn't home.

I lock my bike and cross the street and pass into the narrow outdoor passageway that leads to Madame Sonya's backyard. I've never been to the backyard before, but one day after class Madame Sonya took me and Maria Fabiola to her parlor, as she called it. She had seen something in us, she said, something that reminded her of herself. She wanted us to know that if we were ever in trouble ("I won't ask what kind of trouble, I will never ask") we were welcome to come stay in the shed in her backyard. "It's a safe haven," she said, pointing out the window. "A safe haven?" Maria Fabiola asked. Madame Sonya explained what that meant and told us the combination to the lock that would grant us entry. There wasn't much drama in our lives, and I tried to imagine a time when we might need such a place. Maria Fabiola was probably thinking the same thing. We both smiled gratefully.

The corridor leading to the backyard has cracked cement, a hose spiraled like a forgotten lasso, and a wooden door with a lock. Madame Sonya told us the code to the door's padlock is the year of her greatest fame: 1938. She blames the start of World War II for the premature derailment of her career.

The backyard isn't much of a garden. The large shed takes up most of the small plot of land, and, around it, weeds have grown tall, and in patches, prickly. I step up to the front of the shed. It has a proper door, like to a house. I turn the knob suddenly and push the door open. I want to catch Maria Fabiola by surprise.

She's not here.

The light is on. As I glance around, I think the room looks very familiar. But where would I have seen it before? And then I remember: on the walls of the ballet studio hang photos of Madame Sonya's dressing room in Paris. The interior of this shed is a replica. I know the year this unofficial shrine is commemorating—1938.

On every table of the room stand vases of bouquets of dried roses, fraying ivory-colored ribbons still tied around their stems. Pointe shoes hang from hooks in a row, like Christmas stockings. In the center of the room is a plush pink divan draped with a white fur blanket. I run my fingers over it. The tips of the fur are pointed and hard, as though a substance was spilled on it decades before.

On a wall is a large framed poster. The painting shows a raft holding what looks like a dozen shipwrecked passengers, a few of whom are dead. A boy in the right-hand corner of the painting is waving a red flag, signaling for help from a passing boat. Below the painting the poster says:

The Raft of the Medusa

Théodore Géricault

THE LOUVRE MUSEUM

The shed is windowless, which makes the room feel even more like a shrine to the past. Mr. London assigned us *Great Expectations* last spring and Madame Sonya's dressing room reminds me of Miss Havisham's dilapidated mansion that encapsulated the wedding that never happened.

I pick up the shaggy fur blanket that's draped over the divan. It's almost bulky enough to hide a body. I pull at it quickly, like a magician. There's nothing beneath it except for a tattered and dusty pillow. There's a small bathroom, which means it would be possible to stay here for days without leaving.

I wait across the street from Ballet Russe in the restaurant that sells piroshkis. I ignore the looks of the older Russian women with their bright-red hair. I can tell they don't like that I eat my piroshki with my hands, as though it's a burrito. My sister thinks piroshkis smell like dog food. I think they smell like love. They're warm, the bread is soft, and the meat is a tender surprise. I sit there and wait and watch to see if Maria Fabiola enters or exits the small passageway to the right of the studio.

Eventually the floor-to-ceiling window curtains part and I watch Madame Sonya instruct five-year-olds at the barre. Her pianist accompanies her on the upright. He has white hair and a permanent stoop, as though he's spent his life hunched over at the piano, one ear horizontal to the keys to make sure the instrument has been properly tuned. Madame Sonya turns to him to signal the start of a new song. It suddenly hits me—the pianist is her boyfriend. Why have I not realized this before? Is it because I haven't watched them while eating the piroshki that tastes like love? This revelation that they're a couple provokes a cascade of questions: what else have I not seen? What else could I be missing?

I bike to the beach. It's getting dark and the waves are choppy, their crashes a loud staccato. I walk to the promontory to the right and consider timing my sprint around it so I can make it to the next beach without the ocean splashing or swallowing me. But I'm suddenly scared. What if Maria Fabiola really is missing? I decide to climb up and over the bluff instead. I get to the top and as I'm about to descend to Baker Beach, I look down. From this high-up perspective, I see a figure hunched over, making itself into an oval. "Maria Fabiola!" I yell. The waves crash loudly in response.

I scurry down the cliff and to the sand.

The oval shape is not a hunched girl; it's a rock.

The air is moist, salty. I look down Baker Beach, where a number of bonfires are burning. There's no pattern to their location, their range of brightness.

A burst of white darts in front of my eyes like a comet. It takes me a minute to realize it's a drunk girl wearing what looks like a white nightgown, veering between the bonfires. She has a blanket pulled around her shoulders, trailing behind her like the robe of a dethroned queen. She takes a swig from a bottle and then is chased away by the gathered group of friends as though she's a dog.

The cold breeze hits my face, the damp air rises into my nostrils. The scent of the beach at evening is oddly bosky, like a dense forest.

The girl is now sprinting, trying to get the blanket behind her to rise like a magic carpet. She repeatedly turns her head back toward the blanket, as though to check whether or not it's gathered momentum and height. Her dream, I imagine, is to get on the carpet and fly above all this.

She's running in ovals, and then she looks back and falls over herself and to the ground. She rolls on the sand and at first I think she's laughing but as I get closer to her I hear her wails.

Her hair is spread over her face like seaweed, and one large eye stares up at me. She looks like a dying horse.

"Eulabee," she says. "You know me," and she laughs at her own rhyme.

It's Julia's half sister, Gentle. "Let me help you up," I say. "You're cold. You need to get somewhere warm and sober up." I picture myself, or someone, walking her in circles as she drinks coffee.

"I'm not wasted," she says, slurring the word *"wasted."*

She stands and runs away, the blanket above her head. She zigzags around the beach like a Chinese dragon.

When I leave the beach I bike to Julia's house. I need to tell her mom that I saw Gentle at the beach and that she's drunk.

I ring the doorbell and I see Julia's head peek out from behind the curtain of a window. I ring the bell again. Julia's mom, Kate, finally opens the door.

"Eulabee," Kate says, kindly. "I haven't seen you for a while."

I force a smile. Is it possible she really hasn't heard?

"Yeah," I say. "I wanted to let you know that I was just down at Baker Beach and I saw Gentle."

Her face falls. "What?" she says. "That's not possible. She was home sick from school today. She's up in her room resting." Gentle's room, I know, is in the attic.

"Oh, okay," I say. "It's just . . . I'm pretty sure it was her."

Kate looks at me and I see panic enlarge her eyes. "Wait right here," she says. Her strong legs sprint up the stairs.

I can see Julia in the kitchen eating ice cream out of a carton.

"*Now* you see something," she says. "How convenient for you."

"I thought your mom would want to know," I say.

"Clark!" Kate calls out. "Clark! Gentle snuck out. She's at the goddamned beach."

"Thanks for ruining my family's night," Julia says. "Can you please leave?"

I wait outside the house by the curb in case Kate and Clark need to ask me anything. The side gate opens and they get into a dark green car parked on the street. Julia's mom rolls down the window. "You can go home now, Eulabee," she says impatiently. "Go on home."

14

When I come through the kitchen door it's after 7. My father is pacing, my mother is cleaning, and Svea has the sly smile of a sibling who's confident her sister is going to get in trouble. But my parents are more relieved than angry to see me, and this upsets Svea. While my parents hug me, she races upstairs to her bedroom.

"We were so worried," my dad says.

I expect my mom to temper this comment, but she doesn't.

At dinner—iceberg salad and spaghetti—we talk silently about Maria Fabiola, as though Fate is listening. My parents want to protect Svea, whose eyes are wide—I know she's going to tell her friends about the situation the next day. Her friends have spent the night when Maria Fabiola has spent the night. They know her and now she has disappeared.

The drama extends from the breakfast room table to the study, where, after dinner, my father watches the news. "Greta!" he yells to my mother who's washing dishes by hand. She washes them with great thoroughness before placing them in the dishwasher. "Greta!" he calls again.

She doesn't respond but I run to the study. On the news there's a segment about Maria Fabiola. The camera shows the Spragg campus from an angle I've never seen before—"helicopter," my father explains. Then a close-up of a box of sugar appears on the screen, and for a moment I think it's a commercial break. But the anchorwoman is back in the frame and she's talking about how the missing girl is an heir to a famous sugar fortune. Her great-grandfather started the sugar company and there's speculation that this may be a kidnapping case.

Two questions surge through my mind: A kidnapping? And then: How could I have been her best friend for eight years and not know that her family was part of a famous fortune?

"Did you know that?" I ask my father. "That she was an heiress?"

"Yes," he says, still staring at the television. "Everyone knows that." Then he yells for my mother again. "Greta!" he roars. By the time she arrives the segment is over and my father is angry she missed it. "What were you doing in there?" he says.

"Cleaning up after dinner." Her pink gloves make a *schwak!* sound as she removes them.

My dad repeats everything the news report said so she hasn't missed anything. This is a good lesson for my mom, I think. Next time he calls she'll come running, because he goes over the segment in exasperating detail. He even elaborates on what the anchorwoman was wearing and how her hair was styled. My father never misses an opportunity to admire beauty.

"Did you know Maria Fabiola is an heiress to a fortune?" I ask my mom.

My mom is not easily impressed by appearances or money—in fact, she's skeptical of money so I think there's a good chance this news has escaped her. Otherwise why would she have allowed me to be such good friends for so many years with someone apparently so famously wealthy?

"Of course," she says. "Her mother's from an old East Coast family."

"Her *mom's* the one with money?" I say in disbelief.

"Yes," my mom says. "I think her family came over on the *Mayflower*."

I picture Maria Fabiola's mom in her large sunglasses and the Lilly Pulitzer prints she wears when she takes us to her swim club in Marin. She doesn't dress in what I imagine someone from money would wear. Her jewelry isn't very noticeable and her purses aren't even leather. Instead she carries an L.L.Bean canvas tote bag with her everywhere. She bought Maria Fabiola a similar tote for school. After that, we all subscribed to the L.L.Bean catalog.

Usually I say goodnight and go to my room by myself to finish my homework, but tonight my parents follow me upstairs. After I've changed into an old and pilling Lanz nightgown, they both tuck me in. This hasn't happened since I was nine. I can't remember the last time my dad was in my bedroom—he looks around as though the furniture has moved.

"Can you help me get that sticker off my window?" I ask him. "The one that tells firemen there's a child in this room." I point to the window and my dad lifts up the shade. From inside the room you see the oval of the sticker but not the words.

"Sure," he says. "Tomorrow."

My mom uses her hand to brush my hair away from my forehead. Despite her devotion to the pink dishwashing gloves, her fingers are still rough. She's told me that she's had to add stitches to women's vaginas in the surgery room—especially women from other countries—because they don't want their future husbands to know they're not virgins. These are the same hands that do that, I think. These are vagina-stitching hands.

"How do you feel about going to school tomorrow?" my dad asks. "Do you want to—"

"She's going to school tomorrow," my mom interjects before my father can finish his question. I have never missed a day of school at Spragg. This is what happens when you go to a private school and your parents don't come from money. They have done the calculations of what each day is costing them.

"I feel okay about it," I say. I don't admit that it's kind of exciting with all the television cameras circling campus. I don't say that even though the cameras aren't in the classrooms, some of the teachers have started acting more performative, as though they're being filmed. Especially Mr. London.

"We love you," my dad says, and my mother nods. My mother shows her love in every way possible but has a hard time saying the word. My dad and I have had many conversations about why this might be; we think it's because she's lost so many people she's said the word "love" to. Half her family is dead.

"I love you both, too," I say.

When they leave, I stare up at my tilting canopy, contemplating the fact that Maria Fabiola is the heir to a sugar fortune. I picture her kitchen pantry, which we used to raid after school and on sleepovers. The pantry did have sugar, but I don't remember her parents using it more than anyone else.

When I wake up the next morning my mom's already left for work. My dad insists on driving my sister to school. He wants to drive me, too, but I remind him my job starts today. A neighbor up the street is out of town and she's hired me to collect her newspaper each morning so potential burglars don't realize she's gone. The timing couldn't be better. I want to read the news, to know about Maria Fabiola, but we don't get the newspaper unless the *Chronicle* (the morning paper) or the *Examiner* (the afternoon paper) are running a special trial where you get the paper free for six weeks. These sorts of deals are offered all the time. The newspapers or magazine say you can cancel before six weeks, but they count on you not cancelling. My parents never forget to cancel.

"Why isn't she just putting her paper on hold?" my dad asks. "That way she wouldn't have to pay for the paper, or for you, while she's gone."

"She doesn't trust the newspaper. She suspects the newspaper tells the burglars who's going to be out of town."

"Everyone is entitled to their crazy theories," my dad says, using a shiny black shoehorn to slip on his shoes. From his reaction I can tell that he probably has some crazy theories, too.

I walk out the front door a few minutes before my father and sister leave through the back door. Our street, El Camino del Mar, seems longer today, and steeper. The neighbor's home is nondescript. As far as I know, it has housed neither a magician nor a musician. It's just a regular house in Sea Cliff. The *Chronicle* is on the brick path to the widow's front door. A thin pink-red rubber band is stretched across a photo of Maria Fabiola's face.

I roll the band off and place it around my wrist and open the paper. I know this photo of Maria Fabiola. It was taken of us together at her last birthday party at the roller-skating rink, the one with the multiple posters of Brooke Shields modeling Calvin Kleins. I was standing to the right of Maria Fabiola when the photo was snapped, but I've (obviously) been cut out of the picture. The headline is "Young Heiress Missing." The story starts with some expected adjectives. Our school is "elite," our neighborhood is "tony." But then the word choices become more curious. Maria Fabiola is described as a "star student and devoted ballerina." I don't think Maria Fabiola would want to be described as a star student, but she'll like the devoted ballerina part.

I hear a car horn honk. My first thought before I turn is that it's the man in the vintage white car. But it's my dad. He has Svea and her dour friend in the back seat and encourages me to jump in front. I place the newspaper in my backpack and get in.

"I just wanted to offer you chauffeur service today," my dad says.

When we get to school it seems that everyone's being driven to school by their parents. Some students are getting driven by their families' official chauffeurs. Nobody trusts their kids to walk or take the bus today.

At school everyone's abuzz—no one's acting normal. Teachers ask if I'm okay and don't wait to hear the answer. Throughout my classes, I snap the newspaper rubber band against my wrist to remind myself to act sad. The truth is I don't believe anything bad has happened to Maria Fabiola. This is all a ploy for attention.

During lunch I go to Mr. London's office. The door is propped open with a large dictionary, but still I knock.

"Come in!" he calls out. He's sitting at his desk, with what looks like a student essay in his hand.

"Oh," he says. He looks disappointed that it's me. Maybe he was expecting a journalist.

"Are you busy grading?" I say.

"No," he says, placing it down theatrically. "It's Maria Fabiola's essay on *1984*. I was looking through it to see if I could find any . . . clues."

Now I really know he was waiting for a journalist. He's probably been pretending to read her paper for hours, just hoping someone will catch him in the act and deem him wonderful.

He places the paper down on the desk and I see the grade at the top: "A+." The highest grade Maria Fabiola's ever gotten is a B+ and that was in P.E.

"I was wondering if I could get another book to read for extra credit," I say.

"Came back for more Salinger, eh?"

"No," I say. "Something foreign, maybe. I'm tired of America."

Mr. London turns to the shelves behind him. There's a space where a book used to be—its absence from the shelf is like a missing tooth. I try to think what book it could be. Mr. London runs his fingers over the books' spines.

"Here," he says. "This is a new novel by a Czech writer. I haven't read it yet."

He hands me the hardcover book: *The Unbearable Lightness of Being* by Milan Kundera. The cover is just the title and the author's name in capital letters, no illustration. I read the inside flap to see what it's about. I try not to let my eyes widen because I don't think Mr. London has read the book description. It seems a little racy. "Great," I say before he can change his mind. "I'll read it over break."

"Eulabee," he says as I'm walking out the door. I turn. He's resumed his position, staring at Maria Fabiola's paper. "I know you and Maria Fabiola are good friends. This all must be so hard on you." He shakes his head dramatically. "If you want to talk about anything, my door is always open. Literally. I leave it unlocked."

"Thanks," I say, holding the book to my chest.

"You can leave the door propped open," he calls out.

After school I walk home alone. As I approach my house I see figures seated in the front room. People in the front room can only mean we have company. Studying the backs of the seated heads, I realize Maria Fabiola's parents are sitting on the couch. I freeze for a moment, and then I make a decision. I continue walking, as though my home is just another house in Sea Cliff.

15

I make my way to the Olenska School to check on the shed. I enter the password. The interior feels different today. There's sand on the floor, and in the wastebasket, a packet of Fun Dip. Definitely not 1938, I think. It's obvious that nobody's in the small room at the moment—there's no place to hide—but I still call out her name: "Maria Fabiola?" I say. The name that I've called out a thousand times sounds foreign in my mouth.

I close the door and lock the padlock. I return the numbers carefully to the position they were in before.

On my way out through the narrow passageway, I see an old woman who looks like a witch. I step back. A short squeal escapes my throat. "Eulabee," the witch says. My heart is loud. I stare at this woman who looks like the ghost of someone I once knew. She's wearing a white nightgown and her white-gray hair is coarse and long. "What are you doing here?"

It's the accent that reels me in. It's Madame Sonya. I've never seen her hair in anything but a bun. I had no idea it was so long. I've only encountered her in black leotards and now she's wearing a white nightgown at four in the afternoon.

"I was looking for you," I say, impressed that I don't stammer.

"Why didn't you just come to the studio?" she says.

"I did," I lie. "The door was locked."

She's carrying a grocery bag in her hands. Proof she's stocking the shed with provisions for Maria Fabiola.

"It shouldn't have been," she says, and her Russian accent sounds like she's reprimanding someone—either me or the door itself.

We are still standing, facing each other in the passageway, my foot inside the lasso of the hose on the ground.

"Did you hear about Maria Fabiola?" I say.

"Yes, it's on the news!" she says. "A reporter came here. I told them she was a very talented ballerina." I stare at her. We both know this is a lie.

"What do you think happened?" I say.

"I think she ran away with her boyfriend," she says matter-of-factly.

"What boyfriend?" I say, thinking she will name a name and everything will fall into place.

"I don't know. Doesn't she have a boyfriend?"

I wait for her to reveal more.

"Let me just throw away this garbage," Madame Sonya says.

Garbage. The bag contains garbage. I watch her take it to the taupe trash bin at the end of the passageway. Then she turns, the whip of her white hair following her head a half second later.

I think she might invite me in for tea, but instead she looks me up and down from a distance. My mother has told me not to look at people this way, but maybe you're allowed to do this when you're an old Russian ballet instructor.

"You look skinny," she says. "You've lost weight."

I shake my head. "The scale says the same thing."

"The scale," she says, with a similar disdain that she reserves for speaking of the Nazis, whom she blames for ruining her career.

"You cannot listen to the scale. The scale never tells the truth. I haven't stepped on it for years."

People tell me I look skinny when they want something from me. What does she want from me?

"We've missed you in class," she says. "I am sorry about your friend." She passes by me in the narrow corridor and I back myself up against the wooden fence to make room. A splinter penetrates my calf.

She turns again at the end of the passageway. The low sun hits her nightgown and I can see her pale thin legs through the thin material. "You know there's no class over the holidays, yes?" she says.

Does she really think that's why I came to the studio today? To restart classes?

"Oh, right," I say, playing along, backing away from her like a silent-film burglar. "I forgot."

The comic-book store across the street seems extra busy today, and I peek inside. Could Maria Fabiola be there? If she's hiding out in the shed, she must need books to read. A dozen boys are inside, pretending to browse. It takes me a minute to realize what they're really looking at is the guy from *Mork & Mindy*. He's inside the store, reading a comic book and laughing. The boys and the clerk, a young woman who's the kind of girl that comic store nerds would have a crush on—dyed purple hair, large chest contained (and augmented) by a snug black top—are speechless. The only sound in the store is the actor's laughter. How can he be so impervious to their stares? Maybe he's used to the attention. Maybe he likes it. Maybe he feels most alive when others are looking at him. I try to decide if I feel this way, too.

16

Christmas vacation. School gets out early—the Volvos are waiting in the horseshoe driveway. Even though it's cold out, the windows are rolled down so the mothers can share news about where they're off to for vacation. The next morning they'll leave for the East Coast for family, or Aspen or Tahoe for skiing, or Maui or Lanai for snorkeling and a tan. Svea's going to spend the first week of vacation with her dour friend's mom and the mom's new boyfriend. They're going skiing in Mammoth. I'm not going anywhere.

I spend the days leading up to Christmas at my dad's gallery. I help Arlene file paperwork, and when I have breaks, I open a drawer in the spice cabinet and inhale, before closing it and opening the next one.

In the evenings I walk by Maria Fabiola's house and try to peer in the windows. All the lights are on, all the curtains closed. It looks as though they're living inside a lampshade—figures moving behind linen.

I quickly fall into the routine of waking up and walking up the street to collect the newspaper, reading it to see if there are any updates about Maria Fabiola— there's never anything new—eating breakfast with my dad, helping out at the art gallery during the day, and taking a solitary evening walk around the neighborhood to check on Maria Fabiola's house.

On the fifth day of my vacation, I step into the gallery and immediately notice something's different. The spice cabinet—it's missing. It was there for so long that I never imagined one day it might be gone.

"Where'd it go?" I ask Arlene. My heart is beating fast.

"Somebody bought it," she says. "It was picked up last night after you left." She's gruff when she says this, annoyed that I asked. It's that time of the month.

Svea comes home from Mammoth with a pale neck and a tan from her chin up. When she's asked about her trip, she says it was good, but she noticed her friend could be a bit of a downer, which was a downer. I'm about to express my incredulity that she's never noticed a defining character trait of her best friend before, but I stop myself. There's so much I didn't know about Maria Fabiola until recently.

I join my father in the study to watch the news. Tonight, there's only a brief segment about Maria Fabiola. The same photo appears. Then the anchorwoman talks about the last-minute rush for Christmas trees.

We celebrate Christmas the Swedish way, on Christmas Eve. All day the phone rings—my mother's friends and relatives from Sweden. We eat ham and my mom heats up glogg and even lets Svea and me eat the wine-soaked raisins at the bottom of her small cup. At 8 p.m. we go to church. The service is full of carols and candles. A dark-haired girl dressed in white plays the harp. When it's time to offer up the names of people in our community who are in need of our prayers and support, there are many mentions of Maria Fabiola. My parents utter Maria Fabiola's parents' names as well.

We go home and sit in the front room next to all the straw goats that Swedes put out at Christmastime. I don't really understand this tradition, or the fact that in my opinion the traditional straw figures more closely resemble horses than goats. But now is not the time to ask questions—I'm eager to open the presents under the tree. This takes four minutes because not only do we celebrate Christmas the Swedish way, we celebrate it the stingy way. The gifts are soft so I know before opening them that I've gotten socks and underwear. From the fireplace hangs my Christmas stocking, with my name misspelled as "Ulabee." A family friend gave me the stocking years ago and despite the misspelling, which makes me disappointed in the American educational system, we still use it. The stockings are mostly decorative anyway; tomorrow my stocking will be filled with pencils.

"I have a surprise," my father says. "It was too big to wrap." From behind the piano, he slides out a rectangular-shaped object, the size of a painting. He carefully removes the protective cloth and reveals it is a painting. It depicts kids playing at the beach.

"That's beautiful, Joe," my mother says.

"It's for the family," my dad says.

"Who's the artist?" I say.

"Vanessa Bell," my dad says. "I need to do some research on her."

"Vanessa Bell," I say. "That rings a bell." I don't normally tell jokes like this but my dad's a sucker for puns. I consider this bad pun my Christmas present to him.

"What do you mean?" he says.

"I wrote about her in a paper for Mr. London," I say.

"Did we ever figure out if he's related to Jack London?" my mother asks.

"He's not," I say.

"How do you know?" my mother says. "When I was talking to him he made it sound like he was."

"Exactly," I say. "So he's not."

"Excuse me, Greta," my father says. He turns back to me. "What do you mean you wrote about her?"

"Well, I wrote about the Bloomsbury group and Vanessa Bell was part of it."

I'm greeted by blank looks all around.

"I'll go get my paper."

I run up to my room. When I return downstairs my family is gathered around the painting, staring at it with rapt attention. They resemble the figures in the painting itself—the painting is of three figures surrounding a sandcastle.

I hand my father the essay and he reads it. My mom, sister, and I fold the wrapping paper and decide that most of it will have to be thrown away. It's not crisp enough to save for another present.

"What do you think of the essay?" I say to my dad.

"I think this is exciting," he says. "We might have something here."

My mom and sister put out food for Santa (oatmeal) and his reindeer (carrot sticks) and my dad and I stare into the fire. I don't know if Svea still believes in Santa, but this is not the time to ask.

"I have that feeling," my dad says. "That this might be worth a lot."

"I do, too," I say.

My mother smiles a polite but exasperated smile—she's been through this before. "Okay, dreamers," she says. "Time for bed."

On Christmas morning my mother, Svea, and I put on wool hats and go for a walk along Land's End.

"Just think. Everyone else is still sitting around opening presents," my mother says, gloating as though the goal of Christmas Day is to go on a walk before anyone else.

When we make it back to the house, my father is standing by the front steps, waiting for us. Someone died, I think. I worry it's one of my Swedish aunts. I'm crazy about them.

"Maria Fabiola's on the news," he calls out. "She's been found."

My mother thanks Jesus and God in Swedish.

We run into the TV room without kicking off our sneakers and there on TV I see the headline "Christmas Miracle: Missing Heiress Found Alive." The same photo of Maria Fabiola fills the screen. She was discovered in a blanket on the steps of her family's Sea Cliff home early this morning. The police aren't releasing details about the kidnappers yet, the anchorwoman says. The anchor has a serious expression on her face—the situation requires it, of course—but I can perceive a bit of excitement behind her eyes. Her co-anchor is on Christmas vacation, and she's going to have this story to herself.

"We have to go to her house," my mom says. "We have to welcome her back."

I'm in such shock that I follow after my mom. She's walking fast, fists pumping. My dad and Svea come, too. As we approach Maria Fabiola's house we see a crowd of people, fifty or sixty, standing outside her home. They're gathered as though they're the audience for a performance and the house is the stage.

Neighbors and strangers hug each other in the street. Some wear Santa hats and others wear Christmas sweaters that I doubt are ironic. More people arrive—some by car, some by bike. We wait for something, but we don't know what. Finally, the living room curtains part. Maria Fabiola and her parents come to the window. I hear gasps, followed by a loud silence. Maria Fabiola stares out at everyone in the street. There are cheers and shouts about Christmas miracles.

Her father opens the window. The crowd applauds ecstatically. Maria Fabiola waves a Miss America wave—her arm moves only from the elbow up. She scans the faces in the crowd, taking careful note, I'm sure, of who has shown up to welcome her home. Soon her eyes meet mine. They pause, harden. Then they move on to the other, more adoring faces.

17

When Maria Fabiola was missing, all anyone did was wait for news about what had happened, where she was. Now that she's reappeared, all anyone does is wait for her to reveal what happened and where she was.

A minute before the six o'clock news, my family sits down in front of the television. There are few updates about Maria Fabiola's disappearance except that her kidnappers are said to be Russian. Poor Madame Sonya, I think. She offered Maria Fabiola her shed, and now her countrymen are being thrown under the bus. The anchorman is back—he must have cut his vacation short to cover the kidnapping. Even the anchorman and anchorwoman seem apologetic about how little information they have to report. The man reads a paragraph that goes like this: "The heiress to a sugar fortune has been returned home after what we now know was a kidnapping by Russians. She is recuperating with her family in their Sea Cliff home. We will be sharing more updates as they become available, but right now the family is asking that their privacy be respected."

For the next few nights I sense something strained on the anchorman's face. I imagine he's thinking, I came back early from vacation for this? I came back so I could repeat variations on the same paragraph every night?

On the seventh night of the same paragraph being read aloud, "Sea Cliff home" is changed to "Sea Cliff mansion." "She is recuperating with her family in their Sea Cliff mansion," the anchorman says, his eyes more resentful than ever.

"Mansion?" I say to my dad. "That's got to be good for resale value, right?"

My father doesn't take the bait for a real estate discussion. "Don't you want to call her?" he asks instead.

"No," I say. But later that night I dial the number I first memorized when I was eight. It rings and her father answers.

"Hi, it's Eulabee."

"Hello Eulabee," her father says.

"I want to say how relieved and how . . . happy I am that Maria Fabiola is back home."

"We are, too."

"I'm sure," I say. "I mean . . ."

"She's not taking any calls right now, Eulabee," he says. His voice has always been smooth and calm, like that of a hypnotist. "But I'll let her know you're thinking of her. It will mean a lot to Grace that you called, too." It takes me a second to realize that Grace is Maria Fabiola's mother. Why will she care that I called? Has Maria Fabiola said something to her about me?

"Okay," I say. "Well, say hey to Grace, too. Happy New Year!" I hang up the phone, feeling stupid.

School starts up again the first week of January. On my first day back, I walk to school by myself, the usual way. I see Faith and Julia walking ahead of me. Maria Fabiola's not with them. Maybe she'll arrive late, I think. Like a celebrity.

But when I enter the auditorium for morning assembly I see Maria Fabiola seated in the front row, between her mother and Mr. Makepeace. When assembly starts, Ms. Catanese, the head of upper school, announces that "in light of recent events," the school therapist, Ms. Ross, will now be almost full-time. Ms. Ross bounds onto the stage, wearing glasses and a dress patterned with lemons. "I just want to let you know that all your secrets are safe with me," she says. She pauses, as though about to say something else, but then walks off the stage.

My classmates spend the assembly sneaking peeks at Maria Fabiola, and she spends the assembly staring out the window. I once watched an after-school special where a girl did this when her parents were going through a divorce. With a jolt I realize I saw this special, with Maria Fabiola, at her house.

Ms. Mc. is sick so our classes are combined for science and we have a substitute teacher. Maria Fabiola stares out the window. Midway through class, the substitute walks to the side of the classroom and positions herself in Maria Fabiola's line of view. "How many chromosomes does each human cell normally contain?"

"I don't have to answer that," Maria Fabiola replies.

"Excuse me?" says the sub.

"The police say I don't have to answer any questions that make me feel uncomfortable."

The sub's face contorts itself and her eyes squint for a minute until . . . bam. I can see the very instant that she recognizes Maria Fabiola from the news. Her eyes widen, her posture straightens. "No, of course not," she says. "Of course you don't have to answer that."

Then the sub calls on Stephanie, who lives near Dianne Feinstein in Presidio Terrace.

"Okay, good," the sub says to Stephanie, even though she's gotten the answer wrong. The sub's eyes are still on Maria Fabiola, and she's too distracted by the presence of fame to notice.

As for me, I am invisible.

For weeks after Maria Fabiola's return, a busy, bustling feeling takes over Sea Cliff. The gardeners prune the plants and hedges with more zest and precision, dog owners take their dogs on longer walks, with longer leashes, and the mailman delivers letters and packages with renewed energy, often while whistling an old-timey tune.

I go home directly after school each day so I can intercept the mailman before my mother returns from work. He arrives at the front of the house at 3:15. She usually kickstands her bike in the garden by 3:25. In the wake of my newfound solitude I've contacted several boarding schools and requested applications. I don't want my parents to know that it's my intention to go away for high school. My goal is to see where

I'm accepted and then convince them my life here is intolerable. Application deadlines are approaching so I have to work fast.

It is with his new vigor that the mailman bounds up the steps one day shortly after the New Year with a cream-colored envelope addressed to me. The envelope, with my name written in calligraphy, contains an invitation to a celebration "in honor of Maria Fabiola's safe return." The party is being thrown by her godmother and will be held on a Friday night. I have never personally received an invitation like this before—one that's addressed in calligraphy and contains a stamped postcard for my RSVP. I leave the invitation on the marble table in our entranceway where I place any correspondence I want my mother to see but don't want to personally hand to her. My grade on my Salinger paper, for example.

"Well, this is nice," my mother says. She's standing on the threshold of my room, the invitation in hand. I'm on my bed reading Kundera.

"It's a strange party idea, don't you think?" I ask.

"It's an unusual circumstance," my mother says.

"Yeah, I guess you're right. When you go to the stationery store there's the section for 'birthday' and 'anniversary' but not one for 'return of people who went missing and were suspected to be dead.'"

I smile, hoping my mother will laugh. Instead, she looks at me with a tilted head.

"I want to go," I say. "I just don't really think she wants me there."

"Of course she wants you there."

I stare at my desk as though there's something of particular interest on it. I haven't told my parents that Maria Fabiola hasn't talked to me since her return. She wasn't talking to me before her disappearance either, so that means that it's been three and a half months of silence.

"I think her mom must have invited me," I say.

"Well then you should go for her mom's sake. Unfortunately, we can't make it," she says. "Your dad has a big auction that night—Danny Glover will be coming to the gallery."

"I don't think you were invited anyway. The envelope was addressed to me."

"Oh," she says. "Well, why don't you go mail the RSVP now before you change your mind?"

"Okay," I say. I wonder how she knows this about me—that today I want to go but I'm worried that tomorrow I won't.

"Also, Eulabee," she says. "I've been thinking that now that you're not doing ballet anymore, or dancing school, maybe you want to take some other kind of lessons?"

I stare at the book I've been reading. "I want to take lessons in Czech," I say.

"Czech," she says.

"Uh-huh," I say.

She looks at me as though she's about to say something. But she decides not to. Instead she nods and leaves the room. "Open or closed?" she says about the door.

"Closed," I say only because I want to exert this new power I have over my parents, who are cautious not to upset me.

I read for ten more minutes and then fill out the RSVP postcard. I write my name very, very neatly. There's a small box by "Yes, I will be there to celebrate!" I fill in the box completely, as though it's a multiple-choice test.

As I'm walking to the mailbox I see Keith. He's out by himself on Lake Street, with his skateboard.

"Hey Keith," I call, and he doesn't respond.

Shit, I think. He's turned on me, too. But then he pivots on his board and I spot the bright yellow Walkman case attached to the waistband of his pants and see he's wearing headphones. I get closer and he looks at me and waves. He removes the headphones so they circle his neck.

"Hey," he says. "What are you up to?"

"Mailing something," I say.

"Is that for Maria Fabiola's welcome-back party?" he says, nodding toward the postcard in my hand.

"Yeah, you going?" I hope I don't sound too excited.

"I don't know. I'll check with my parents when they get home. I think we're supposed to go away that weekend for a wedding."

"Where?"

"Yosemite."

"In the winter?"

"Yeah. We're not camping. We're staying at this hotel. The Ahwahnee."

"The Ahwahnee? That's where they filmed *The Shining*."

I expect him to say "Cool," the way most guys would, but instead he shares my response. "That's a little scary," he says.

I nod.

"Don't you think it's kind of weird to have a party for her?" he says. "I mean, I'm glad that the kidnappers brought her back but it's just . . . I mean what's going to happen at the party? Will there be party favors?"

"Maybe they'll give out blindfolds," I say.

He stares at me for a second. My sense of humor really is not for everyone. Then he smiles. "Or maybe they'll give out suitcases of cash."

"Was there a ransom?" I ask. "Did her parents pay?"

"I don't know," he says. "But why else would she suddenly be returned home?"

"How much money do you think?" I ask. "What's the going rate?"

"For a heiress, a lot." He pronounces it like hair-ess.

I consider sharing my theory that she wasn't kidnapped at all, that she planned her own disappearance, but I decide this isn't the time. I don't have enough proof; in fact, I don't have any. Besides, I'm tired of Maria Fabiola being the only topic of conversation. It's been that way for months. Even when people are talking about other things, they're talking about her. When my parents ask me what time I'll be home, or when teachers wish us "a safe weekend," it's all because of her.

"What are you listening to?" I ask.

"The Furs," he says. "You like them?"

A few months ago, I would have lied and pretended I knew a band even if I didn't. But I want things to be different now. I want to be different now.

"I don't know them," I say.

I expect him to scoff, to say "You don't know them?" But instead, he removes his headphones from around his neck and places them over my hair. He presses "play" on his Sony Sports Walkman and I hear a raspy British voice singing about swallowing tears and putting on a new face.

I remove the headphones and hand them back to him.

"You don't like them?"

"No, I do like them. A lot." I can't tell him that the reason I'm giving the headphones back to him is because the song has moved me so much, so instantaneously that I'm afraid I'll start crying right then and there.

"They're really good," he says.

"Yeah," I say. There's an awkward beat. "I guess I'll mail this now," I say, holding up the postcard.

I'm up late that night reading *The Unbearable Lightness of Being.* It's a scene with a bowler hat—Sabina is naked in her Prague apartment seducing Tomas with her body and the hat. I try to imagine what a bowler hat looks like. I decide I'll search for one next time I'm thrift-store shopping in the Haight. When I'm thrift-store shopping in the Haight *alone,* I think. I feel sorry for myself and then I feel sorry about how sorry I feel. To pity oneself is to reach a new low, I think. I write down those very words in my diary. Reading Milan Kundera, I've decided, is good for the brain. It's made me a philosopher.

It's after 11 p.m. when the front doorbell rings. I sit upright in my bed. The front doorbell rarely rings unless it's someone selling something. Most of our friends come through the back door.

I walk out into the upstairs hallway and peer down below. My mother is talking in Swedish to a blond woman. I only see the tops of their blond heads, leaning in close but speaking loudly. Something bad has happened. I've been around enough of my mother's friends and through enough Santa Lucia performances to understand a good deal of Swedish, but I'm not fluent. I keep hearing them say the word *mjolk*, which means "milk," and milk doesn't seem to warrant the intensity of their discussion. Or the presence of the two suitcases.

I descend the stairs and theatrically rub my eyes as I step onto the landing, making sure to trip in my fake-slumberous state. Maybe I'm a born actress, I think.

"Oh no, did we wake you?" my father says.

"It's okay," I reassure them.

I look up at the blond visitor as though just taking note of her presence. "Hello," I say. "Who are you?"

"I'm Ewa," she says. "It's spelled with a 'W' but here you say it like a 'V.'"

"I'm Eulabee," I say. "I haven't yet figured out how to introduce myself so people remember."

"Oh, I can help you with that," she says. Her English is fluent, with a slight British accent. She went to good schools. And she's much younger than I first thought. When I saw her from above she looked round, approaching middle age. But now, standing across from her I see that she must be in her early twenties. She must be . . .

"Ewa is an au pair," my mother says. I knew it.

"I *was* an au pair," Ewa says.

One of my mother's unofficial duties as part of the Swedish network is being an advisor to au pairs from Sweden. They're given my mother's number in case something comes up. In this case, something clearly has come up. My mom and Ewa resume speaking animatedly in Swedish.

My father shifts from one slippered foot to another. He clears his throat. "Excuse me. Does anyone fancy tea?" he asks. My father doesn't speak any other languages than English, and in the presence of foreigners, which, in our house, usually means Swedes, he subconsciously takes on a British accent and a thing for tea.

"Is it decaffeinated?" Ewa asks. My parents look at each other. It's clear it's never before occurred to them to check whether the tea they drink late at night is caffeinated or not.

"I'll check," my father says, and goes to the kitchen. He's often domestic in the presence of beautiful women. Ewa, while not straightforwardly beautiful, is captivating, with her round, wide face and strangely (for San Francisco in winter) tan skin. She's plump, curvy. She's wearing the white pants that all Swedes love. In America women with her body type probably wouldn't wear white pants. Maybe it's a mind trick, I think. By wearing white pants she's signaling that she's not heavy, even though she is. Her eyes are the violet-blue of a flame and her shoulder-length hair is curly. Maybe a perm, I think. My Swedish cousins are all getting perms.

My mother and Ewa talk for a minute and the only words I understand are *Damernas Värld,* which is the name of a women's magazine. I know this because we have old issues stacked in a basket in our bathroom. Whenever Swedes living in America go "home for the summer," they bring back as many *Damernas Världs* as they can carry.

"Oh, we should speak English with you," Ewa says, evidently disapproving of the fact that I don't

speak fluent Swedish. Swedes always disapprove of this fact.

"I'm learning Czech," I say.

My father returns with a tray of tea and we follow him into the front room. I know that my parents have a high regard for Ewa because we never sit in the front room this late at night. It's cold here, with all its windows.

"So," I say with fake casualness. "What brings you here?"

"I spilled some milk," Ewa says.

My mother elaborates. "Ewa was an au pair for a neighbor on Lake Street. The older girl is named Maxine." My mother stares at me. "Do you know her?"

"What school does she go to?" I ask.

"The Viner School," Ewa says. "She's in eighth grade."

Viner is the other all-girls' school. We compete against each other sometimes in sports, and always for boys. We have many choice things to say about Viner girls.

"I think I do," I say. I don't add that I met Maxine before she dropped out of dancing school and that she has a reputation.

"Maxine's a little . . . confused but has a good heart," Ewa says, "but her father . . . it's a different story. Tonight, he was getting a late-night snack and spilled a whole gallon of milk on the floor. He called out to me because my room is by the kitchen. He ordered me to clean up the milk."

"That's not her job," my mother says to me.

"No, that's not in my job description. If one of the younger kids had spilled the milk that would maybe be my job, but my job is not to clean up after him."

"Why was he drinking milk?" I ask.

"That's beside the point," she says.

"Right," I say. Her response confirms my hypothesis that he wasn't drinking milk, but something stronger. Why else would she say it's beside the point? I also suspect she was not in her room but was drinking with him. But it's not my position to offer my theories here, now.

"I think you should go back to bed," my mother suggests.

"Okay," I say. "See you tomorrow."

I lie sleepless in my canopy bed, and an hour later, I hear my father placing Ewa's two suitcases down in the room next to my room, which is called the playroom, though no playing happens there. The furnishing is too formal, the room too neat. There's a fold-out leather couch, peach in color, where guests spend the night. It's a strange layout for a guest bedroom because I have to pass through the room to get to my room. Now I hear Ewa getting settled into the bed. The springs of the couch sigh. She sighs. She and the couch sigh together.

In the morning, I walk quietly past Ewa. She's moved the mattress to the floor, and she's sleeping facedown, her arms and legs at diagonals, like an "X," her white pants hanging on the golden doorknob.

18

When I come home from another day of my classmates ignoring me, Ewa is sitting in the guest bedroom, beading.

"What are you making?" I ask.

"Earrings," she says. "Do you have pierced ears?"

"Yeah, I have two holes in my left ear, one on my right. I did the second hole myself."

"Wow," she says. "That's brave."

"I have an ear-piercing business," I say. "I pierce people's ears. Boys, girls, whoever, with ice and a sterilized needle." *Business* is a grand word for what I do. I have pierced three ears at the rate of $5 each. One of them was Maria Fabiola's.

"I'm impressed," Ewa says. "And that's good that you sterilize the needle."

I knew she'd like that part. All Swedes are devotees of sanitation and sterilization.

"Maybe you can pierce my ear sometime. I'd like to go for a third hole." She pulls on her right earlobe and shows me where she'd like it.

"That would look good," I say.

I watch her slip a light blue bead onto a wire. I wonder what her plans are now that she's not an au pair anymore.

"Do you have a boyfriend, Eulabee?"

"Not at the moment."

"Is there someone you like?"

"Yeah."

"Then you should make him your boyfriend."

I let out a quick laugh. "How do I do that?"

"Well, first you should go on a date. Is there anything you two have in common? Something you both like?"

"We both like music. We both like this band called the Furs."

"The Psychedelic Furs!" She stops beading.

"Yeah," I say, hoping this is the same band.

"I just saw that they're playing in San Francisco soon."

"Really?" I say.

"Yeah, you have to get tickets and invite him."

"I don't know," I say. "That seems a little . . . like a big leap."

"Here's what I'll do," she says. "Why don't I buy two tickets and then you can tell him that you have an older friend—it's always good to have an older friend, sounds impressive and makes him realize how mature you are—and your older friend happened to have two tickets to the Furs show and she gave the tickets to you."

I feel a lightness in my chest and in the arches of my feet. "That would be really cool," I say. I stare at Ewa, this refuser of cleaning up milk spills, with a new admiration.

The following evening, I find two tickets on my desk fanned out in a "V" shape. The concert's at the Fillmore. I've never been to the Fillmore. My lungs push against my rib cage. Now I just have to invite Keith. And then convince my parents to let me go. And I have to find out if the band's recorded more than the one song I heard half of.

I change out of my uniform into my best black jeans. I tie a black sweater around my waist as a makeshift belt. I pick out a blue long-sleeve with a big button at the top. Good, I think, glancing at the mirror on the back of my door. I don't glance too hard, just enough to think it looks nice. Closer examination, I have learned, is not my ally. I place Band-Aids on my ankles to prepare for the pulling on of my Doc Martens, which have not been sufficiently worn in yet. Doc Martens are for evenings and weekends. They are not permitted at Spragg.

I walk to California Street to take the first of two buses to the used record store I like. I hope to see Keith on his skateboard but he's not there. I wait for the bus and then take it for four blocks before I decide to get a transfer ticket from the bus driver. It's not a bus with boys. I hold my transfer in my hand and wait fifteen minutes for the next one. It's worth the wait. On this bus I see Axel Wallenberg. He doesn't know me, but I know who he is because he's Swedish, too—our moms know each other. Axel Wallenberg, I have decided, is a deep, beautiful boy.

While his beauty is obvious, his depth may not be immediately evident. But I'm sure it's there because I know a secret about his family. I've been obsessed with Raoul Wallenberg ever since I wrote an essay on him last year in seventh grade. He helped save hundreds of Jews in World War II by traveling from Sweden to Hungary and providing Jews with fake Swedish passports. But then in 1945 the KGB in Russia imprisoned him. The Russians say he was executed in 1947 but his body was never found, and I'm not sure I believe them. A lot of people don't. I personally suspect that Axel Wallenberg, who's currently on the 1 California bus with me, is his grandson.

We switch buses at Presidio and take the 43 to the Haight. Axel and his friends are in the back of the bus and I'm seated in the middle. I have to make sure to turn the pages of *The Unbearable Lightness of Being* so it looks like I'm actually reading the book, in case anyone's checking, which they are not. I'm focused on the boys' conversation, which is now about Maria Fabiola. More interesting to me is the fact that Axel is talking about how he's going to go to the party to welcome her back.

"You should totally spike whatever they're serving," one of his friends says.

"Yeah," says the other friend, the one with the longer hair. "You should spike the punch."

As we near Haight, I look out the window and see a girl with mousy hair wearing a pink fur jacket, round glasses, and bell-bottoms. She's talking to two much older men, one with high heel boots. The other man is wearing a brown leather jacket and a beanie.

"Check it out," one of Axel's friends says. "There's that freak who was swinging naked from the monkey bars."

The other boys look out the window. "Fucking Chelsea morning," Axel's other friend says.

"She's so messed up," Axel says. "But I feel bad for her. Her mom abandoned her and went to Africa."

India, I want to say. But I don't want them to know I've been listening to their conversation.

When we get to Haight, we all get off the bus. The boys go left, where shops sell pipes, and, near the park, dealers sell pot. I turn to the right, toward the bigger stores. I pass a few high-school dropouts with dogs. You can tell they went to fancy summer camps at some point—they still have those sailing bracelets yellowed and rotting away on their wrists—and now they're sitting outside stores, asking for money.

The record store is filled with guys, all of them about five years older than me. I only see one other girl buying records, but she's with her boyfriend. I flip through the used records and can't find what I'm looking for, so I have to go to the NEW section. And there it is—the Psychedelic Furs. There are two records. No, three. I don't know which to get. I decide I can only afford one. Svea's birthday is coming up in March and I need to save the rest of my money to buy her something that I'll find deep in her closet a week later.

I choose the most recent record, with the image of a man with reddish hair in a blue tuxedo jacket. I hold it between my hands like it's the face of someone I love.

The balding guy at the cash register with the ironic? Blondie shirt nods when I give him the album. "Cool choice," he says, and I don't say anything because *thanks* doesn't seem like the right response. I try to make my eyes say *Of course*. Then I carry my bright yellow record bag down the street, taking care to not swing my arms so it doesn't hit anybody.

I pass a mannequin in a storefront window wearing a dress that's black with tiny white polka dots. Impulsively, I enter the shop.

Two willowy women work at the store. One of them is wearing a scarlet bow tie, the other a pencil skirt with a bronze zipper that runs all the way down the front. "The dress in the window . . ." I start to say.

"Oh, that would look fabulous on you," says the woman in the bow tie.

"That's our only one," says the woman with the zipper skirt. "I'll take it off the mannequin."

She approaches the window and removes the mannequin. For a moment she and the mannequin are engaged in an awkward dance. Then the woman lays the mannequin on the floor of the shop and starts to unbutton the bodice of the dress. It looks like she's about to perform CPR. The inert form, I can't help but notice, looks remarkably like me. The bow-tied woman observes this as well. "The mannequin looks a little like you," she says.

"I just hope I look more alive," I say.

"You do," she says.

"Well, that's good!" I say. The two women stare at me. Then the one on the floor manages to wrestle the dress off the mannequin. She hands it to me. "The dressing room's that way," she says. "Behind the pink curtain."

In the dressing room is a poster of Botticelli's *Birth of Venus*, with Venus rising up out of a half shell, and maybe the poster has something to do with it, but when I put on the dress and look in the mirror, I imagine I look like a better version of me. A future me. *This is what I'll look like when I'm older*, I think, and this reassures me. Maybe I am meant to wear dresses with small polka dots.

"Let's have a look," one of the women says.

I exit the dressing room, hoping the spell holds.

"Wow," they both say, and I know it has.

"You have exactly the right body for that dress," Zipper Skirt says.

"It's not too low-cut?" I ask, hoping she won't say it is. I know it's on the cusp of revealing too much.

"Definitely not," she says.

"If you've got it, flaunt it," Bow Tie says. And this makes me laugh. I've never had, never flaunted.

"Do you happen to have a bowler hat?" I ask.

The two women look at each other, then shake their heads, and look at me. But my request for another item has inspired them.

"Do you need shoes?" Bow Tie asks. She's wearing very high heels.

"I think I can just wear these with the dress," I say looking down at my Doc Martens.

"No!" they both cry out in unison.

"What size are you?" Zipper Skirt asks.

"Six and a half," I say.

"Okay," she says, searching the shelves of shoes.

"Try these. They're used." The shoes she offers me are silver and delicate—the opposite of my Doc Martens.

I sit on a low velvet couch and change shoes. The Band-Aids are falling off my heels, and I have to push them back into place. Then I stand, trying not to wobble.

Bow Tie whistles.

"I wish I could whistle," Zipper Skirt says. "But I can't. It's genetic."

I look in the mirror.

"See how nice they make your legs look. They're e-lon-gated," Bow Tie says, elongating the word itself.

"I'm afraid to ask how much everything is." And suddenly I'm very afraid.

Zipper Skirt gets out her calculator and presses some buttons and then tells me the total including tax, which is substantial, but not as much as I feared. I have enough money with me, all of my Svea birthday money. If I spend it, I will only have three dollars to my name. I know I can run errands for the old people in the neighborhood and earn it back. I pay, and the dress and the shoes are delicately wrapped in tissue and then stuffed ungracefully in a paper bag.

I thank the women and step around the inert and naked mannequin on my way to the door. A bell rings as I exit the store.

I get off the bus one stop early so that I can walk past Keith's block. He's there, on the street, on his skateboard. And he's alone. I walk toward him, trying to be casual. I make sure my record bag is facing him.

"Hey," he says.

"Hey."

"What'd you get?"

"The Furs," I say.

"No way."

"Yeah," I say. "And guess what? I have this friend who's older and she gave me two tickets to their show."

"Seriously? Cool."

"Yeah," I say. I stand there, gathering up the courage to say what I say next: "Do you want to come?"

"Pardon?" he says. He says "pardon" instead of "what" and I love this about him—like he's from the South or the past or both.

"Do you want to come with me?" I repeat. "I have two tickets."

"Maybe," he says. "When is it?"

I tell him the date and he says he'll check with his parents later and let me know.

"Cool," I say. Before I can mess anything up, I turn away. I hope he's watching me as I walk down the street with my record, my dress, my shoes, and the three dollars I have left to my name. I feel a loosened Band-Aid release itself from my ankle and fall off, but I don't turn around to pick it up. I don't care about litter because I am immortal.

19

At dinner I bring up the concert.

"I think it's a good idea for you to go," my mother says.

I know she means *I think it's a good idea for you to have a new friend your age.* She likes that Ewa and I get along so well, but I can tell she's worried that the phone never rings for me anymore.

"Wait a second, Greta," my dad says and puts down his fork. He turns toward me. "You're going to a concert with a boy?"

"It's not a boy," my mom says. "It's Bonnie and Fred's son. You know, from Sea View."

I think of correcting my mother. Keith *is* a boy. But pointing this out won't help further my case.

"What is this band all about?" my dad asks.

"They're British," I say.

"I'd like to hear them before I agree to anything," he says.

"Okay. I have the album."

After dinner, Ewa helps my mom with the dishes and my dad follows me upstairs. He bought me a record player from Sears last year. Embarrassed, I covered up the Sears logo. I used a special handheld machine that lets me punch out capital letters on red embossing tape. I wrote "BRAND NAME HERE" on the tape and stuck it over Sears.

My dad sits in my desk chair, swiveling. I hope he doesn't see the concert tickets—I don't think he'll like the fact that I'm the one who invited Keith to the show.

My dad is no stranger to concerts. He went to see Little Richard across the bay in Richmond when he was in his twenties—he was one of two white men in the audience, he said. But there are noticeable gaps in his career as a music lover. One time I asked him who his favorite Beatle was. "I kind of missed that trend," he said. *Missed that trend*, I thought. *The Beatles trend*. So I don't know what he'll think of the Psychedelic Furs.

The record's already on the turntable and I place the needle carefully on "Pretty in Pink." I figure the title of that song is innocuous, and makes the band seem most appropriate for someone my age.

He closes his eyes as he listens to the song.

"Eulabee," my dad says.

"Yes," I say.

"They're fine," he says.

"Okay," I say. "So . . ."

"You may go to the concert," he says, though it's clear he can't believe he's saying the words. "We'll have to work something out where maybe Ewa picks you up right afterward or something."

"Of course," I say. "Thank you."

Instead of saying, "You're welcome," he nods. Then he stops swiveling and stands.

Ewa drives us to the show in my parents' yellow Saab. Keith and I are quiet on the drive and Ewa fills the air by talking about how popular heavy metal is in Sweden. We pull up in front of the Fillmore. The crowd is thick and older.

"She's cool," Keith says when Ewa drops us off.

"Yeah," I say. I love that he likes her.

The scent of damp fallen leaves hits me as we enter the building.

"Pot," Keith says.

Right, I think. The only other concert I've been to is Duran Duran.

We're standing in the middle of the theater, not knowing what to do with our hands. Everyone else around us has drinks in theirs. When the concert starts, we sway a little to the music.

"No banter," Keith says.

"What?" I ask. Leaning in to him, I smell Tide. His mother must not dilute the laundry detergent the way my mom does.

"Interesting that there's no banter from the band. Not even 'It's so great to be in San Francisco.'"

A relative newcomer to this world, I say, "Yeah."

The band starts playing "Heaven," and Keith begins spinning around with his arms stretched up in the shape of a V.

"What are you doing?" I ask.

"That's what Richard Butler does in the video for this song."

I know better than to ask who Richard Butler is. I never thought of learning any of the names in the band.

"Try it," he says.

I start spinning, reluctantly at first.

"Stretch your arms up and out," Keith says.

I do.

And there we are spinning, circling in opposite directions so that our hands gently collide with each rotation. Each time we face each other I see that Keith is singing the lyrics. I succumb to the music. I soar up above the world and nothing else matters except seeing Keith's face again on the next rotation, when I get another whiff of Tide.

"I'm so happy we came to the concert," I say.

"What?" he says, trying to hear me over the music.

"I'm so happy," I yell.

When the Furs finish their set and leave the stage my heart drops. But then everyone shouts for an encore—me included, me especially—and the band comes back out and plays "Pretty in Pink." I scream because now I know what it feels like when the music stops, and I desperately don't want it to end.

When the show is officially over, Keith and I step outside into the cold fog. The night air smells like new leather jackets. The Saab's low and wide head-lights come toward us and we both slip into the back seat.

"How was it?" Ewa asks as we drive away.

"Fantastic," Keith says. His fingers spider-walk over to my hand and he holds it. I feel his heartbeat in his thumb.

"Look at this," Ewa says as we drive up Pine. "The lights must be timed. We're hitting green lights the whole way." As we cruise smoothly and steadily through the night, it feels like we're on a boulevard built only for us.

20

The Friday of the party finally arrives and Maria Fabiola's not at school. Maybe she was kidnapped again, I think, but know better than to say this aloud. The only person I could say this to would be Keith. He would think it was funny. But Keith's out of town, in Yosemite, for his cousin's wedding.

No one can concentrate at school—not even the teachers, all of whom, except for the science teacher, Ms. Mc., are going to the party, too. Everyone's distracted by what exactly is going to happen. Is an announcement going to be made? A secret revealed? Not one of us knows any more about the circumstances surrounding Maria Fabiola's disappearance and her miraculous Christmas Day return than we did three weeks ago.

Class is dismissed even before the 3 p.m. bell. The mothers in the horseshoe driveway are out of their Volvos, standing in small knots of conversation. They look more dressed up today than usual. I count at least six ironed pencil skirts.

When I get home I walk through Ewa's room to get to mine. We call it her room now because the Swedish network hasn't found her a new au pair position yet. This is a huge relief to me.

I've shown Ewa the polka-dot dress I bought on Haight Street, but she hasn't seen it on me. I close the door to my room and slip it on for the party. As I button the bodice I think of the shopkeeper with her delicate, capable hands working the same buttons on the mannequin. I don't feel like myself, in the best way possible, since myself is someone who's been ostracized.

I slide into the new shoes and step into Ewa's room.

"Perfect," she says, pronouncing it *purr-fect.* Then, instead of asking me to spin around, she gets up from the couch and circles me as though I'm a statue at a museum, a work of art.

"Now," she says. "I have a surprise for you."

She walks to the sewing closet, her wide feet leaving imprints in the plush white carpet. She has transformed the sewing closet into her own—my mother's knitting, embroidery, and quilt square have all been moved to the bottom shelf. I take this as a welcome sign that she'll be staying for a while.

Ewa removes a circular leather case that looks like it's intended to carry a musical instrument—a tambourine? A drum? She unzips it with the easy efficiency of a flight attendant demonstrating how to use a flotation device.

"Ta-da," she says, and she hands me a hat.

It takes me a minute.

"Is this a bowler hat?" I ask. When reading *The Unbearable Lightness of Being* I hadn't been able to picture it.

"*Ja*," Ewa says. Swedes aren't big nodders. They do the opposite of nodding—they raise their chin up and inhale and say *ja* at the same time.

"Yeah?" I say. I try it on and know it is probably ludicrous.

"*Ja, ja*," she says, seeming noncommittal about the success of the hat she has purchased for me.

I wear it anyway. Ewa and her au pair friend Monica drop me at the party in the Jaguar that belongs to Monica's "family." They can't find a parking space so they double-park outside the house so I can exit. I hold on to the back door handle a moment too long so that I'm

still holding it when they start driving away. *Release,* I
tell myself. *Let go.* I half-hoped they'd walk me to the
door.

The party is at the home of Arabella Gschwind,
Maria Fabiola's godmother, a woman I haven't met but
who my dad says is a well-known interior decorator.
"She did the living room of the Decorator Showcase
house this year," my dad told me, clearly impressed.
Arabella lives in the Marina. Correction: she lives *on*
the Marina. She lives on the street that borders the
water where boats are docked and where everyone runs
on the weekend, looking fit and pretending to live in
Southern California. Marina Boulevard is the street in
San Francisco known for its Christmas decorations. Just
last month, in December, my family took a special trip
to drive by the houses with all their lights and reindeer
and Santas. "Pick your favorite one," my father said, as
though whatever house we chose would be ours.

"Too much," my mother said. "Too much . . .
America." But her posture revealed the truth—she was
tilting forward in the front seat to get a better view.

It's windy out tonight. As I climb the stairs to the
house I hold on to the top of my bowler hat, afraid it's
going to blow away. I'm relieved I don't have to ring
the doorbell; the door is unlocked and cracked open.
When I step inside it slowly occurs to me that this is the

home of Leon, that Arabella is his mom. Leon went to the French-American school last year until his parents divorced and he moved to Geneva to live with his dad. I know Leon from dancing school. Everyone knows him from dancing school. Last year, when we wanted to tease fellow classmates, we'd call their houses when we knew they weren't home and when their parents asked if they could take a message we'd say, "Tell them Leon called." Then we'd spell the name so there could be no confusion. We knew that when the girl returned home she would be thrilled. We imagined her calling Leon's house and feeling rejected. That was our idea of fun.

The walls of the foyer are filled, salon style, with photos of Leon at all ages. Here he is sporting ironed shorts with suspenders. Here he is dressed in a suit and bow tie. *Poor Leon*, I think—such fancy clothes for a kid. I spot a woman across the room dressed in a tight white silk dress, a bolero jacket, and heels so high I worry her calves might snap. I suspect she's the reason for Leon's old-man wardrobe. A face-lift has never been pointed out to me before but the skin around her eyes and mouth is so taut that all I think when I see her is *face-lift!* She's greeting a young man. "I'm Arabella," she says, and kisses the young man on both cheeks. Astonished by the attention, he fails to introduce himself. "Where's the toilet?" he asks. "The W.C.," she corrects him, "is to the right of the Diebenkorn." He walks away from her, feigning comprehension.

I hear the party within the heart of the house—in the living room and the dining room to the left of the foyer—but I can't bring myself to join. The front door opens and Julia and Faith step inside. I look at them, expectantly, plaintively. *We're all here. It's all okay. A new year. A party. A safe return.* But their made-up eyes slide over me.

I check my watch. It's 6:50. I have two hours and forty minutes until I'm picked up at 9:30. I think of a three-hour job I had passing out flyers last summer. The flyers were for a camera store that would develop three rolls of film for the price of two. The flyer was your average flyer—black and white and the word "Special!" written in red. I was instructed to stand downtown, a block away from the camera store, and to give the flyer out to anyone who passed me by. "Except homeless people," I was told. "They don't have cameras."

I stood on the corner and tried to hand out flyers. Most women ignored me. Most men took a flyer. But even fifty minutes into the job I could tell I was failing. My feet hurt, I was bored, and I still had three hundred flyers to go. I needed to pee, so I went into the closest hotel, the St. Francis, and took the glass elevator up to the top floor. After determining the restroom was empty, I stuffed fifty flyers in the trash can. I could have gotten rid of the whole stack, but I felt funny. So I stood outside the men's restroom for ten minutes until I was sure it was empty. Then I stuffed sixty flyers in the trash can of the men's restroom. What a relief, I thought. I walked out of there with sheepish pride.

That's what I feel like at Maria Fabiola's welcome home party, like I have to figure out a way to dispose of huge swaths of time. I carefully prepare myself a plate of food that I eat very slowly and then with abandon so that I can get another plate later, which will take up more time. I pause thoughtfully and at length in front of each of the framed paintings. These paintings are in a different price range than the paintings my father's gallery sells. I even spot what looks like a Chagall at the top of the stairway, but I can't get close. The stairway is cordoned off with a burgundy velveteen rope, as though the home is an historical estate offering tours.

For the first hour of the party I don't see Maria Fabiola. I see girls from my class, who nod politely, dismissively, or else pretend they don't see me. I speak to Ms. Livesey for a minute and wait for her to compliment my dress, but she doesn't. Then Julia and Faith start talking to her and they act like I'm not standing there so I float away from them and toward Mr. London, who's eating a chip filled with guacamole. I tell him I'm enjoying the Milan Kundera novel.

"More than Salinger?" he asks, dipping another chip, this time into a bowl of salsa. I nod, not wanting to get into Salinger with him again, and then excuse myself to use the restroom. I see boys from dancing school, which I dropped out of months ago, but I don't see Maria Fabiola. I circle the party in a way that reminds me of the shark at the aquarium in Golden Gate Park, going around and around. Eventually, I'm sure everyone can see that I'm doing laps, so I fill my plate up with food for the second time. Most guests are congregated in the main dining room. I find a small and unpopulated study on the other side of the foyer.

I sit in the corner of a red velvet couch—it's the kind of couch that makes you sit up really straight. The coffee table is glass and stacked with enormous books about fashion—Coco Chanel, Diane von Furstenberg, Carolina Herrera. I wedge my glass of seltzer between two large books and hope it won't spill. The food is good—risotto—and I dig into it.

I smell him before I see him. Polo by Ralph Lauren. It's Axel, and he sits next to me on the couch. He's with two friends who follow him into the study and sit in the two chairs on the other side of the coffee table. They put their heaping plates of food on top of the coffee-table books. A roasted red pepper slowly droops onto a book about Bauhaus, but they don't seem to notice. I recognize one of the boys—he was on the bus with Axel that day, but I don't know the other one. The boy from the bus is just over five feet with fine features and tan skin. The other boy has light brown hair that's gelled attentively, and acne only on the top of his face; the bottom half of his face is clear. I speculate that the hair gel might be causing the breakouts on his forehead and wonder if anyone has told him that. The pecking order is immediately clear: Axel is in charge, and then comes the tan guy then gel boy.

They don't say hello to me and so I continue to eat. I have a forkful of risotto halfway up to my mouth when the gelled boy says, "Hey, that rice looks like my cum." The other two boys turn to stare at me. My fork hovers midway between my mouth and the plate, but I know better than to eat it now. I put my fork down.

"Is it your cum?" says the tan boy.

"Yeah, maybe you saw Maria Fabulous and came all over the kitchen."

Maria Fabulous, I think. That's what boys called her. Of course.

"So are you going to eat it?" the gelled boy asks.

"Your cum, no?" I say. "The risotto, yes."

Axel laughs and stares at me. He does that double-take motion where I can tell he's just noticed that at a particular moment, from a specific angle, I can look pretty. "You're the Swedish girl," he says. I think of myself as Czech, not Swedish, so it takes me a minute to respond.

"Yep," I say.

"I thought so," he says, proudly, as though he's just solved a mystery of great importance. "Our moms are friends."

"Really?" I say, trying to be nonchalant. My mom talks about Axel's mom in a reverential way. She's so wealthy and does so much for the Swedish community (all of her good deeds are commemorated by polished plaques), but my mother knows better than to call them friends. This is something I admire about my mother: she never exaggerates a social connection.

"How can you be Swedish and not have blue eyes?" the gelled boy says.

"Ignore him," Axel says. "I like your hat, by the way."

I check his face for sarcasm and see none. "Thank you."

I lift a forkful of risotto to my mouth.

"How is it?" Axel asks.

I'm still chewing.

"Are you going to spit or swallow?" says the tan boy.

"Dude, drop it," says Axel, and turns toward me. "What's your name again?"

"Eulabee," I say.

"Eulogy?" says the gelled boy.

"Ignore both of them," Axel says. His full body is turned toward me now, both his knees almost touching mine. I can smell his Polo by Ralph Lauren but there's also another smell, almost cardamom-like, beneath the cologne. Alcohol, I realize. He's drunk, all three of them are, or else they're on their way.

"What are you drinking?" I ask.

Axel smiles. He has the kind of smile that reveals the man he's going to become. I see it clearly. He is destined to sell high-end real estate—his photo, with that same smile, will be featured in a little box on laminated full-page, heavy-paper stocked flyers for Pacific Heights mansions.

"Give me your cup," he says. I oblige. He reaches into the inside pocket of his suit jacket and turns away from me theatrically.

After five seconds he swivels toward me once again.

"Ta da," he says and holds the cup out to me.

"Dude," says his gelled friend. "You should never ever become a magician."

I close my eyes as I down the contents of my cup in one long, long gulp.

"Oh, shit," one of the boys says.

I look at Axel, who now appears less like a future real estate magnate and more like Milan Kundera.

Suddenly, I hear a triangle, like the kind played at a symphony. Reluctantly I turn away from Axel's beautiful face.

It is a triangle.

Arabella is holding the triangle and striking it with a wand. She pauses to allow the sound to reverberate throughout the house. She's removed her bolero jacket—most likely to show off her toned arms as they hold the triangle. Her white dress is even snugger than I imagined. She's not wearing underwear.

"We are gathered here today—" she begins.

"To celebrate this thing called life," Axel's tan friend says.

Arabella owls her head toward the study. I suspect she's going to call him out for disrupting her speech, but her eyes are on Axel. I realize she thinks it's Axel who's spoken. And clearly, she likes Axel. A slow and possibly seductive smile creeps up on her orange-lipsticked mouth.

"Exactly," she says. "We are gathered here today to celebrate life. And one life in particular. We are so grateful that our beautiful friend, my incredible goddaughter, has been returned to us."

"Amen," some adults whisper loudly. The girls clap. The boys whistle.

Maria Fabiola is still nowhere in sight.

"Maria Fabiola's mom was my roommate at Vassar," Arabella announces. "That was before . . ."

The doorbell rings and the entire crowd turns, expecting to see Maria Fabiola. Lotta, the Dutch girl enters, looking hesitant. She's wearing a red flannel skirt, a bright yellow tank top, and a purple coat. Everyone looks disappointed that she's not Maria Fabiola; Arabella looks disappointed to have such a terribly dressed guest. Arabella turns away abruptly as though wishing to erase the sight of her. Lotta's eyes search the room and lock with mine. She wants to come sit with me, I can tell. But Axel's alcoholic concoction has warmed my body and sharpened my mind and I see her for the traitor she is.

I deliberately dart my eyes away from hers. I turn them to my empty red cup and then to Axel, who mistakes the flight pattern of my eyes to mean that I want a refill. I don't need one, but I appreciate that he's been watching me closely enough to think that's what I'm signaling. When Arabella resumes speaking, Axel plays the part of the bad magician. He turns away, reaches into his left suit pocket with his right hand as though about to extract a sword, but instead refills my red cup from what I imagine is an engraved silver flask.

"Calgon, take me away," I whisper into his ear. Axel leans toward my mouth so that my lips inadvertently graze his upper earlobe. Even though I can't see his face, I feel his body tense in pleasure. He returns the red cup to me.

We've missed whatever else Arabella has said. When I turn back, everyone is silent, their eyes on the stairway.

Maria Fabiola steps down the first rounded stair. Audible gasps emerge before we can even see her face. She's wearing a long white wedding dress. She looks like the photos of debutantes in the *Nob Hill Gazette*. I watch as her white satin–heeled shoe takes a step around the curved staircase and then her body turns and she's facing the crowd. She looks stunning, and five years older in the best possible way. Her hair is styled in a bun with highlighted tendrils framing her face. It dawns on me that she's spent the day in a beauty salon—that's why she wasn't at school today.

She takes another step down, and then her serious face with its hazy gaze absorbs the appraisals of everyone in the crowd. I suspect she's counting the number of people who have shown up for her—115, 120. When the room is silent, she breaks into a smile, and extends her hands diagonally in front of her, as though she's just finished an incredible performance—a dance routine, or an aria with a high note. The party guests all break into applause.

When the clapping and whistling, finally, begins to wane, Maria Fabiola's mother and father walk down the stairs so that they're standing on either side of her, but one step above. Has the entire evening been choreographed like an awards ceremony? How did her parents know to halt their descent one step above hers? I am impressed.

Arabella strikes the triangle again and Maria Fabiola begins to speak.

"I want to thank you for all your support while I was missing," she says. Her voice is soft and her tone shaky. Her voice, I decide, is part of the performance. "Now I know a lot of you are wondering what happened . . ."

The guests laugh and then quickly quash their laughter, sensing that it's not appropriate. "Well, I'm not at liberty to tell you all the details right now because I promised ABC News an exclusive." She's rotating toward the far left, the middle, and the far right as she speaks, and bowing subtly. She reminds me of Glinda, the Good Witch, speaking to the Munchkins. "But I can say that I was kidnapped by foreigners and that they took me on a boat. At first, I wasn't treated well—I almost died in the dark!—but one of the shipmates took pity on me and then they started treating me better. The ship crashed near an island, and it was then, when I swam to the island, that I was able to escape."

The guests start clapping.

My head feels light. I bite my own tongue with the left side of my mouth. I'm afraid I might say something. I might object, like a bad guest at a wedding interjecting something horrific during the ceremony.

Her father makes a brief, bland speech about how happy they are to have her back. Her mother thanks Arabella for throwing a party in her beautiful home. Arabella uses this acknowledgment as an opportunity to announce, "My ex-husband may live in Geneva, but our divorce was anything but Swiss. Everyone took a side. But at least I have this house." More laughter.

Then she strikes the wand against the triangle once more—a sign, I suppose, that the performance is over. Maria Fabiola turns and ascends the staircase. Her dress has a scallop-edged train, and it swiftly recedes like an ocean wave.

"You think she got a boob job?" Axel's tan friend asks.

"She was kidnapped," Axel says.

"Well maybe they made her get a boob job," the gelled friend says.

"It's the dress," I say. "It does that."

They all nod, as though I'm the expert on dresses. I pick up the Diane von Furstenberg book from the coffee table to cement my new reputation.

"You want to go outside?" Axel asks me. "I know a secret balcony. Leon took me there once."

"Sure," I say. I follow him to the back of the study. I can feel my classmates' eyes on him, on me, on us. I try to disguise my pleasure, but the corners of my mouth lift up against my will. He opens the door that looks like it would lead to a utility closet and I trip over the threshold.

"Watch your step," he says belatedly and we both laugh. I'm on my knees on the balcony. He helps me up and clumsily, I stand. I've never been drunk before but I'm pretty sure this is what it feels like. A tumbling, hilarious, warm feeling. A cocoon against the world. A cocoon with only me and Axel inside.

The balcony is small and looks out on the marina. The view is socked in with fog. Against the white sky the black upright masts of the boats look like the measure bars on a sheet of music. The sun has set and the night air is damp and refreshing against my skin.

"Don't fall over," he says.

"I'll try not to," I say.

He reaches into the inside pocket of his suit once again and takes out the flask. Except that now I see it's not the silver flask I was envisioning. It's plastic. "Is that a shampoo bottle?" I ask. "The kind you get for traveling?"

He shrugs and pours some of the golden liquid into my red cup. I take a sip, and suddenly, now that I know the flask isn't what I thought it was, that it's sold at the drugstore next to the miniature deodorants, my drink tastes soapy.

Axel pours himself the rest. The shampoo bottle is empty, and he screws on the plastic top and returns it to his suit pocket.

"What'd you think?" I say, looking out at where the view of the bridge would ordinarily be on a clear night.

"Of what?"

"The talk on the stairs."

"Oh," he says, as though that was a side note to the occasion of the party. "It was a lot more official than I thought it would be."

He shifts to his other foot. "What'd *you* think?" he asks, slurring.

I want to say that I think it was ridiculous, that Maria Fabiola is lying, that I think all of this is a scam, a big story to get attention and that she was really in a shed behind a ballet studio. But I look at Axel, who hiccups, and I know I can't tell him any of this. For a brief moment I wish he were Keith. Keith would understand. Keith would be in agreement with me and, I'm pretty sure, wouldn't share my suspicion with anyone else.

The wind blows, and I hold on to my hat. I smell his cologne and the warmth that is in my throat and in my stomach now is on my skin. I inhale deeply. We're back in the cocoon together.

"Do you want some more?" he asks. I nod because I want whatever he is offering. I want him close, especially now that we're outside and the Polo scent is diffused and, I imagine, surrounding me. I hope my dress will smell like Polo tonight, tomorrow, the coming week. I want to share the scent with Ewa. I imagine holding the dress up to her nose so she can inhale, and then waiting for her verdict, which I know will be appreciative. Ewa, I decide, is the best thing that's happened to me in months. Until now. Until Axel, who is leaning in toward me, his lips coming for mine. Something happens when he kisses me though—I think my lip is bleeding, or maybe it's his, but something tastes like batteries. And then my brain registers what his mouth is doing—it's transferring the alcohol from his mouth into mine. I swallow it and step back and he smiles at me, and I force myself to smile back at him when the truth is that I feel disappointed. I wanted a real kiss, not the drink he's forcing from his mouth into mine.

I lean back into him and push my lips against his. I want the connection again, I want the cocoon. He places both hands on my breasts and squeezes. Then he looks down at his hands, squeezing, and smiles at his hands as though he's proud of what he's doing.

"Touch me," he says. I touch the back of his neck, even though I know that's not what he means. "Touch me down there," he says.

I put my hand on the bulge beneath his pants zipper. I look out onto Marina Boulevard to make sure no one can see us. They can't. The street is startlingly empty. A lone dog walker, a group of French-speaking tourists drinking beer out of bottles. *Merde*, one says.

Axel places his palm over the back of my hand and guides it up and down—not in the direction I would have moved it; I would have gone left to right. I want his hands back on my breasts. I don't know how we suddenly got to me standing with my hands on his crotch on a balcony at a party. It's like we've forwarded a VHS tape to the middle of the movie after only watching the opening credits.

But this is the position we're in—his hand on my hand on his crotch when the balcony door opens. I hear the swell of laughter coming from inside, along with festive music. It's Arabella. She steps up and out onto the small balcony. Axel and I promptly release ourselves from each other.

"Love at first sight," she says.

"Good evening, ma'am," Axel says, and I'm impressed how quickly he knows to do this, to revert to normal party talk.

She studies him. "What a handsome boy," she says with the authority of a queen about to knight someone. Her bolero jacket is back on, her wand and triangle out of sight.

Then she turns her gaze toward me. Reflexively, I smile, as though a photo is being taken, as though a compliment is about to be bestowed upon me.

"Aren't you cold?" she says, studying my bare arms, the scoop of my dress's neckline.

"No, I'm very warm blooded," I tell her.

"Well, I can certainly see that!" she says.

Axel convulses, suppressing a laugh.

"I came outside to let you know that dessert will be served in the next ten minutes."

She steps back down into the living room, closing the balcony door behind her.

"That was hilarious," Axel says.

"Maybe for you."

"I think she's just upset because she wants me and Maria Fabiola to date. Tonight was a setup I think."

What? I want to ask. But I don't want this moment, like everything else, to be about her. I want to rewind, to back up. Suddenly, his hand dives down and I think he's falling. His fingers reach under the hem of my dress and snake up my thigh.

"Oh," I say. And then I say nothing. The breeze on my legs is damp, and between my legs I feel a rush of moisture and heat. Axel's hand is moving toward that wet heat. His cologne is closer to me now, which is all I care about. Except that the concoction is making me ill. The strength of the cologne and the alcohol and the revelation that he's being matched up with Maria Fabiola are whisked in my stomach. His finger is inside me and then maybe two fingers are inside me.

"Wow," he says. "You really like this."

I don't know how to respond because I don't really like this. He pulls his hand out and even in the late-dusk light I can see that his fingers are stained with . . .

"Blood!" he says. "Jesus Christ. You're bleeding."

We both stare at his fingers and for a moment I think he's done that to me, he's made me bleed.

"Wait, you're not . . . are you getting your period?" he says.

"I don't know," I say. "Maybe." Maybe this is why I'm sick to my stomach.

"Maybe? Why didn't you tell me? What am I going to do with this?"

I stare at his hand. "Here," I say, and lift up my hem and turn the inside of the dress toward him. "You can wipe it here."

He does.

"You're gross," he says.

"Your grandfather would be so disappointed in you!" I yell.

"My grandfather?"

"I know your grandfather is Raoul Wallenberg!"

"Who? What the . . . ?" he says. "You are batshit nuts."

Then he turns and steps back into the living room.

I decide to wait fifteen seconds to follow him so it's not as obvious that we were outside together. My stomach feels like a cardboard box being taped up too tight. When I finally step back into the living room, I hear Maria Fabiola's favorite song, "We Are the Champions," being played too loudly. Tiramisu has been served. Maria Fabiola's nowhere in sight. The bathroom is locked, so I stand outside it. I remove the bowler hat from my head and hold it in front of the skirt of my black and white polka-dot dress as casually as I can. Just in case anything has leaked through and I'm showing. When the bathroom opens up I clean myself off with wads of toilet paper that I dispose of in the toilet, where the tissues bloom in size. The water turns pink and I flush. I rummage under the sink for pads before I remember that Arabella has no daughters.

At 9:20 I go outside to wait for Ewa and her friend. As I'm standing there waiting I realize I've forgotten my hat inside the house, possibly in the bathroom, but I can't go back. When Monica and Ewa pull up they don't stop and park, they just pause. I'm so grateful to see them that I jump into the back seat and Monica starts driving. "How was the party?" Ewa says.

I start to answer her—I've already planned to lie— but a force greater than words twists inside of me and I vomit all over the back seat of the Jaguar.

21

When we get back to the house, Ewa sits me down at the kitchen table and makes me tea and toast.

"It's decaffeinated," she tells me, as though this is something that I would be concerned with at the moment. My only goal is keeping the toast down.

My parents are out at their auction and won't be home for an hour. An enormous blessing. I have no idea how they'll react to me getting wasted at the party for Maria Fabiola.

My heart is rattling against my ribs, my ribs are rattling against my heart.

"How do you feel?" Ewa asks.

"Betrayed."

"By who?" she says.

"Whom," I say.

"Who?"

"I feel betrayed by my femininity."

"I wish I had something wise to say right now," she says, and looks at me with mercy and pity. I can tell she thinks she's seeing herself as a young woman. I let her stare. Her eyes scan my hair, where a strand of vomit hangs like tinsel.

"The best advice I can give you is to take a shower, shampoo well, and go to bed," she says. "I have extra pads in the cabinet behind the mirror if you need them."

In the bathroom, I see someone who looks like me but is paler and bloated. In the bathtub's soap dish I spot Ewa's razor that she uses to shave her legs, and probably her armpits. I've never shaved any part of myself. There are three mirrors—a triptych—that cover the medicine cabinet. If I arrange them a certain way—with the mirrors on the left and right facing inward, they produce a thousand reflections. I pick up the razor and stand on top of the toilet, so I can see the multiple me's.

My pubic hair is darker than my hair. It's curly and, I decide, unruly. I take the razor and push as hard as I can and swipe it left and right over the small mound of my pubis.

Then I start screaming. The blade is filled with hair and there's more blood. First the blood emerges in tiny, multiple drops, then gushes. And the burning sensation is unbearable. I leap down from the toilet seat, jabbing my toe against the sharp edge of the bathroom scale. I run to the shower. The water pressure helps. A pool of pink circles my feet and I step off the drain. I press a washcloth against my pubis—pressure is the only thing that helps.

It's suddenly clear to me that I wasn't supposed to push the razor so hard against my tender skin. It also occurs to me that I was supposed to use soap and water, that that's why razors are often seen on the soap dishes of bathtubs.

I start sobbing in the shower. I cry and cry until the water turns cold. Then I cry because I'm freezing.

Outside the bathroom door, I hear Ewa screaming. "If you don't unlock this door in one minute, I'm knocking it down."

I turn off the water and crawl to the door and let her in.

"I'm sorry but I think I destroyed your razor," I say.

The next morning the sharp pain wakes me. I feel like I'm on fire. I sit up. I have a headache, but the pain coming from between my legs is so intense that it makes my headache seem minor.

Ewa has left aspirin outside the door to my room. I swallow two without water and the chalkiness of the pills makes me gag.

When I make it downstairs I find my father lying flat on the dining room table. He's covered with a white sheet like he'd dead, but I know he's alive because Ewa is humming while giving him a massage. The protective padding is on the table, which is a good thing, because we never use this table for casual dinners. But apparently we use them for massages.

"I was just telling your father that maybe you should walk on his back," Ewa says to me. "I'm too heavy, but you would be the right weight."

"Okay," I say. I know I'm going to have to be agreeable, to make amends to everyone in the house.

The front doorbell rings. Maybe it's another Swedish au pair on the run, I think. I open the door and Maria Fabiola is standing before me. She looks so much smaller than she did last night, so much more my size now that we're on the same level and she's wearing jeans instead of a dress. But her fury is huge. Her fury is a force I can feel before she opens her mouth.

"That was my party and you ruined it," she says.

She puts her bag down on the brick entranceway so I can tell she plans to stay.

I step outside and close the door behind me. I don't want my dad and Ewa hearing this.

"I don't know how I ruined it," I say. I don't remember throwing up until I got into the Jaguar, but I don't volunteer this information.

"Seriously? All anyone can talk about is how you got blood all over Axel. He's told everyone."

"Why would you even want to be set up with someone like him?" I ask.

She screams a scream of frustration instead of answering. Even her hair, which has lost its hair-sprayed hold, is extending out from her head like exclamation points.

"I don't know how you managed to make last night about you, but you did," she says.

"All I did was get my period."

"That's disgusting."

"You know what's disgusting?"

She stares at me. I don't know what I'm going to say is disgusting so I drag out the moment while I plot my response.

"The story you told," I say. "You really think anyone's going to believe that kidnapping story?"

"Excuse me?" she says.

"Have you taped your ABC interview yet?"

"They've done B-roll," she says.

I nod as though I know what that is.

"That means they've filmed me walking on the beach with my family. I think it turned out really well."

"You could get in a lot of trouble for lying to the news," I say. I don't know if this is true, but it sounds true. "The story you told last night has a very familiar ring to it, don't you think?"

"What do you mean?" she says, and I can tell she's frightened.

"*Kidnapped*? Robert Louis Stevenson."

"What are you talking about?"

"Oh my god," I say, as it dawns on me. "Last time I was in Mr. London's office there was a book missing. It was *Kidnapped*, wasn't it? You took it."

"What are you talking about?" she says in a quiet voice.

"The book. You got the idea from a book."

"I don't even read books," she says. "Maybe the kidnappers do, but I haven't exactly been able to read recently since I was busy being kidnapped!"

"Well, I'm just saying that before you go on ABC and give them your exclusive, you might want to revise your story a little bit."

"I'm leaving," she says. "But I brought you something you forgot last night." She reaches into the bag and takes out my bowler hat. She throws it on the ground between us. Then she proceeds to jump up and down on it like it's a fire she's trying to stomp out. "There," she says. She turns and walks down the stairs. I pick up the hat and try to restore its shape, but it's destroyed. I carry the hat inside like it's a once beloved animal that I'm going to need to bury.

22

On Sunday morning my dad comes into my room and asks if I want to go to church. I pull the covers over my head.

When my parents return home, I learn that my mom talked with Julia's mom, Kate, in the church courtyard. A plan has been hatched for me to go to Julia's house this afternoon to make Valentine's Day cards.

"It will be just like how it used to be," my mom says. "You girls used to always make cards together."

I tell her we haven't made valentines since we were little.

"Well, Kate misses you," my mom says.

"Well, Julia hates me."

My mom wants to contradict this. She opens and closes her mouth. After a few seconds she says, "Anyway, it's all been arranged."

My mom makes a cheesecake and pours red cherries from a can on top, spreading them with a wooden spatula. Shortly before 3, she walks with me to Julia's house, carrying the cheesecake, which has been Saran-wrapped. She's taped down the edges of the wrap with the rough surgical tape she brings home from the hospital.

Kate opens the door wide, an exaggerated gesture to show how welcome we are.

"Your new house is beautiful," my mom says before she even looks around.

"Thank you," Kate says. She seems genuinely grateful for the compliment. She's still wearing her church clothes, which resemble her shiny ice-skating outfits except that the top is less sparkly and the skirt is slightly longer.

"I brought you a cheesecake," my mom says and offers the cake to Kate.

"Thank you so much, Greta. You know how much I love your desserts. What was that thing you made for the bake sale last year?"

"Broom cookies," my mom says proudly.

"Exactly," Kate says. "Do you actually place them on a broomstick to get them to look like that?"

"Yes," my mom says. "But don't worry—it's a clean one!"

They both laugh fake laughs.

Julia is not within sight, and we all stand in the entranceway, waiting for her without saying we're waiting for her. Sitting by the door are three boxes with "Hitachi" and "Toshiba" and "Sanyo" printed on the side.

"New TV?" my mom asks.

"It's a long story," Kate says, and sighs dramatically. I can tell she wants to share this long story, but my mom doesn't prompt her. "Anyway, the short version is they're for sale. Do you know anyone who wants to buy a TV, a Betamax, or a karaoke machine?"

"Maybe," my mom says. She seems genuinely interested. "How much are you selling the Betamax for?"

"Um, I'll have to get back to you about that," Kate says.

"Jesus, Mom," Julia says as she enters the room. "Gentle will go even more crazy if you sell that stuff."

"Don't call your sister crazy," Kate says.

"Hi Julia," my mom says. "I like your hair."

Julia's normally light brown hair has turned orange. I know this is the result of the Sun In she sprays on her head. She goes crazy with the Sun In.

"Thanks," Julia says. "I was sitting outside with lemon in my hair."

She's a terrible liar. It's winter and it's been over-cast.

"Well, it worked!" my mom says.

The two mothers stare at each other for a moment—it's time for my mom to go. "I'll make sure Eulabee's back before dinnertime," Kate says. "And thanks again for the cheesecake." I know she won't eat it because she's constantly worried about having a bubble butt. She says all ice-skaters get them.

After my mom leaves, Kate shows Julia and me the valentine-making station she's set up for us in the dining room. This is what she calls it—a station. Construction paper, scissors, sequins, beads, stickers, and glue have been set out for us as though we're nine. There's even a packet of Scooby-Doo valentines from some other decade.

"You know what all those boxes are about?" Julia says when we're alone.

I shake my head, and try not to show my relief. I'm so glad we're going to talk about the electronics boxes and not about Maria Fabiola's party.

"When Gentle's mom took off she went to this ashram."

"I thought she went to India," I say.

"Yeah, the ashram's in India."

I don't ask what an ashram is.

"She started this love affair with the head guy and now she's basically considered the queen of the ashram."

I make a sound to show I'm impressed.

"I know, right?" Julia says. "Anyway, since she's the queen, guess who's the princess?"

"Gentle," I say, with authority.

"Exactly. So the members of this ashram treat her like a princess and they give up all their money and buy her all these presents. All these . . . things."

"They just send them here?"

"Yeah, boxes just arrive all the time. Gentle hates it. She thinks it's *horrendous*. She calls it 'eighties commercialism.' Anyway, I'm tired of everything being about Gentle all the time."

We both stare at the valentines on the table. I can feel Julia retreating from me again, like a wave.

"I have an idea," I say. "Wouldn't it be funny if we sent all the teachers valentines from other teachers saying how much they loved each other?"

"What do you mean?" Julia says, leaning a little bit forward.

I suggest we make one from Mr. Makepeace, to Ms. Mc., the science teacher.

"*I wanna talk dirty to you—in my stupid British accent*," Julia says.

I laugh. She writes it down. This is good, I think. She likes me again.

"We need one from Mr. London to Ms. Catanese," she says.

"*I love you—literally,*" I say.

Julia laughs, then pauses, as if realizing she didn't get the joke. I lunge ahead to erase the awkward moment. "Ms. Ross should get one from that therapist who filled in for her that semester. Mr. Gunji."

"She was having personal issues," Julia notes. "Faith says she got a breast reduction."

"*I miss your boobs,*" I say. "*Love, The Gunj.*"

We snicker for a good two minutes.

"Ms. Patel needs one from Mr. Makepeace," I say. "Actually, everyone should get one from Mr. Makepeace."

"Even the men?"

"Especially the men."

We decide Mr. Makepeace's should all be Scooby-Doo. On each one we write "*R-roh! I love you!*"

Then we add, "*Love, your Boss.*"

From Mr. Robinson, the gym teacher, to the sewing teacher: "*I want to run away with you. But not too fast, because I'll be wearing my long pants designed for the Outback and they make it hard to run.*"

From Ms. Mc. to Mr. Robinson: "*When I watch instructional videos about the reproductive process, I think of you.*"

From Mr. London to Ms. Catanese: "*How about a threesome? Franny, Zooey, and you? Oh, and also me. So it'll be a foursome.*"

From Ms. Peterson, the math teacher, to Ms. Trujillo, the Spanish teacher: "*Me + you = Amor.*" We look up the Spanish word for "sex" in a pocket dictionary, and we paste *Sexo* over *Amor*.

We laugh for an hour, but eventually, when we decide every teacher should get at least one from at least two other teachers, it becomes an oddly workmanlike process. We use all the supplies Julia's mom has set out: metallic pens and stickers with googly eyes. No one is spared except for Ms. Livesey. She won't fall for it, we decide without debate.

When we're done, we place them all in a black garbage bag that we think won't look suspicious. I stand up and stretch and while feeling very proud of our creativity and work ethic, I smell something foreign. I wonder if Kate's burning something—she's a terrible cook.

But it's Gentle. She's descended from her bedroom, which is in the attic. The smell, I realize, is her patchouli. Her hair is parted in the middle, but other than that she looks disappointingly unlike a hippie today. She almost looks normal.

"Why are you guys working in the dark?" Gentle asks.

"It's not dark," Julia says, glancing up at the chandelier.

"Just open the curtains," Gentle says, moving toward the window.

"No!" Julia says.

"Who cares if you can't see the bridge from this house?" Gentle says.

"My mom cares," Julia says.

"So she's going to pretend there's a bridge out there? Toto, we're not in Kansas anymore."

"Were you planning on going out?" Julia says, hinting.

"Yeah, I'm going to go donate some of these boxes," Gentle says.

"The boxes have things in them," Julia says. Her eyes look intensely blue. They get that way when she's worked up.

"Yeah, that's why I'm going to give them away."

"I think Mom was planning to sell them," Julia says.

"Well, they're mine," Gentle says.

"Did it occur to you that Mom might *want* to sell them?" Julia says. She doesn't use the word *need* in front of me. She's already embarrassed enough about their relative poverty.

"They're not hers to sell," Gentle says. She picks up the biggest box. "Can you get the door, please?" she says to Julia.

"No, I'm busy," Julia says, holding a small, dark sequin up above the side of her mouth, like it's a beauty mark.

Gentle puts down the box, opens the door, picks it up again, and leaves.

Strangely, the scent of her patchouli is stronger once she's gone.

"Let's go check out her room," Julia says and jumps up from the table so abruptly that the wooden floors shudder.

To get to Gentle's room you have to take a ladder to the attic. "It was her choice to live up here," Julia says, climbing up ahead of me. "Attics are where a lot of nutty people live. They feel at home there with the bats."

The rungs of the ladder are half circles and hard on my hands and bare feet. As I ascend, the smell of the incense grows stronger. I prepare myself for the mess

I expect is waiting for me at the top of the ladder. I picture beads hanging from doorframes, a waterbed, bell-bottoms, and platform shoes tangled on a shag rug—vestiges from wherever last night's adventures took her.

But Gentle's room is surprisingly neat. It's neater than my room. "Do you have a housekeeper?" I ask Julia.

"Not anymore," she says, slightly out of breath from the climb. She gets out of breath surprisingly fast for an athlete. She's at the ice rink four afternoons a week.

A Grateful Dead poster is framed. The floral-patterned teacups set out on her desk look more British than Haight-Ashbury. Poor Gentle, I think. She's failing even at being a hippie.

"I have to show you something hilarious," Julia says. She opens Gentle's top desk drawer carefully and extracts a ledger of graph paper. "She keeps a chart of everything that was better in the seventies than the eighties."

The line down the middle has been drawn with a ruler. The pencil writing is extremely neat.

"Isn't that hilarious?" Julia says. "I mean, who keeps lists like this?"

1970s	1980s
Pillows on floor	Chairs
Fondue	Churros
No watches	Watches
Free love	No love
Records	Cassettes
Tie dyes	Ties

"Let's write her a valentine," I suggest.

"Who should it be from?"

"The seventies."

"Ha!" Julia says. We descend the ladder, return to the dining room, and get to work. We use all the beads. *"We miss you!"* we write, *"Love, All the dirty hippies."*

It's dinnertime, and I know I should leave. Julia and I are friends again and I feel very tall and brilliant. On my way home from Julia's I take a small detour and walk past Keith's house. The lights are off, the car gone: he's still in Yosemite. After dinner and before bed I sneak out of the house while my mom's doing dishes and my dad's in the study. There's still a Christmas wreath hanging on the door of Keith's house, and the lights are on, but it's too late to knock. I circle the house, hoping he'll see me. I make all the calculations—he'll see me crouching in the bushes, late at night, and he will love me. He will come out and I'll tell him all about the wonderfully witty and subversive valentines I made with Julia, my friend again.

23

At Monday morning assembly I hear my class-mates' whispers. *Blood. Axel. Party. Slut.* Every-thing happens very fast. I am untouchable. No one can quite believe I've shown up for school after bleeding all over a boy at Maria Fabiola's celebration. The disgust surrounds me like a sulfurous fog. Julia walks right by me without saying hello.

By the end of first period, boarding school seems more necessary than ever. Weeks ago, I submitted my applications and enclosed cash as my admissions fee. I ironed the bills so they would look like adult money. All that's left for me to do is request teacher recommendations—no small task. Ms. Livesey's will be good, but two of my top choice schools require letters from an English teacher. At lunch I go to see Mr. London.

His door is propped open even wider today. He takes a deep breath when he sees me—his cheeks deflate as he inhales.

"I wanted to let you know my plans," I say, sitting down in the chair on the other side of his desk. "I'm applying to boarding schools for next year."

"Yes, you mentioned that," he says.

I know I haven't mentioned this to him, because I haven't mentioned this to anyone, not even my parents. But now is not the time to correct him.

"Well, these boarding schools require a recommendation from my English teacher, and I was wondering . . ." I pause, hoping he won't make me finish my sentence, but he doesn't say anything, so I'm forced to complete it. "I was wondering if you would please do me the honor of writing a recommendation. I respect your time and know it's a favor, but I would be very grateful."

He stands and looks out the window, with his hands behind his back. This is the pose actors assume in movies when playing a president making an important decision about the future of their country. It is not an appropriate posture to take on when deliberating about whether to write a teacher rec for an unhappy student.

Finally, he turns back around. "I can do that for you, Eulabee. I can do that, but it will be a challenge for me."

"I'm sorry to hear that," I say.

"It will be a challenge because I don't feel that you and I have respect for the same books. We have different taste in literature."

"Isn't that allowed?" I ask.

"Not in my class," he says.

Now it's my turn to take a deep breath. I think of Thatcher, a boarding school I'm applying to that gives each student their own horse. *Do it for the horse*, I tell myself.

"I'm sure we can agree on certain books," I say.

"Like which ones?"

"You haven't read the Milan Kundera book yet, have you?"

"No," he says. "A student has borrowed my copy so I haven't had a chance to."

"I'll bring it back," I say.

My eyes scan his bookshelf, searching for a book he and I can discuss. I know better than to pick one by Jack London.

There it is, back on the shelf. *Kidnapped* by Robert Louis Stevenson. "How about *Kidnapped*?" I say.

"A student just borrowed that without checking with me first," he says. "It was missing and then returned."

"It was *kidnapped*," I say, hoping he might smile.

He doesn't smile. "No, it was missing."

I shrug in a way I hope is endearing.

"Has anyone ever told you that you have an . . . unusual sense of humor?" he asks.

"No," I lie. "You're the first."

"Did you take the book?" Mr. London asks.

"No, I already read it a few months ago."

"What did you think about it?"

"I think it's very . . ." I stall, figuring out how to best finish my sentence. "I think it's very pertinent to today."

"How so?" Mr. London asks.

"Well, you were at the party Friday night." I look away. I hope he didn't see me at the end of the evening.

"Yes," he says. "So?"

"Nothing," I say. I am careening toward self-sabotage and can't stop myself. He looks at me and I go over the waterfall. "Don't you think that what Maria Fabiola said she experienced had strong echoes of the Stevenson book?"

"Let me think about that," Mr. London says. And then he puts on his thinking face—his eyes go up toward the beige ceiling and he scratches his jaw.

Finally his eyes descend. He's done thinking. "I'm not so sure I see the parallels," he says.

"You don't see the parallels?" Already I'm sure he will not write my recommendation.

"Well, she was kidnapped, but it wasn't in the Scottish Highlands," he says. "And the Robert Louis Stevenson book was published a hundred years ago."

How this man is teaching literature is a miracle, a debacle.

"But the whole bit about the boat and almost dying and the island and escaping from the island?" I say. "And the kidnapper who convinced the others to be nicer to her?"

"Sometimes writers get at very deep, underlying currents that make them timely for generations," he says. "I'm glad you're seeing some of the more superficial themes."

"Can I take a break for a second?" I ask. "Get some fresh air?"

"Sure," Mr. London says.

I stand and walk outside his office. My forehead is sweating, my earlobes are hot. How is it that Mr. London can't see that Maria Fabiola stole her story from Robert Louis Stevenson? Mr. London gave us a lecture about plagiarism a month ago. It was surprisingly cogent for him.

I find myself pacing outside the office, counting to 120. The fluttering of gossip is louder now—I hear it coming from down the hallway. *Blood. Slut. Booze. Stupid hat.*

I reenter Mr. London's office. I remove the teacher reference forms from my backpack and go to place them in his in-box, to the right of his desk. *What the hell,* I think. On top of the in-box I see a familiar red envelope waiting to be opened. I didn't think Julia was going to follow through on delivering the valentines. I want to snatch the red envelope but Mr. London is watching me.

"I know we don't see eye to eye on everything," I say. "But I am poor and have only my dreams. Tread softly, for you tread on my dreams."

"Are you plagiarizing Yeats?" he says.

"I'm quoting Yeats," I say. "*Quoting.*"

"You should acknowledge your sources," he says.

"Everyone should acknowledge their sources," I say, and walk out.

24

After school I walk past Keith's house, but he's not outside on his skateboard. I ring his doorbell. No one answers the door, but this doesn't mean no one's home. I hear footsteps inside, running to the back of the house. They're what I imagine webbed feet sound like on a hardwood floor.

As I walk home I see my mom on her bike, but she doesn't see me. She's on her way back from work, and I view her the way a stranger would. *That is a determined, beautiful woman,* I think. A Swedish farm girl riding a bike on a San Francisco street lined with palm trees.

I arrive home five minutes later. My mother is pulling something out of the freezer. She's still wearing her support hose, the stockings she wears at work to keep her legs from swelling. She spends most of the day in surgery, standing. The stockings are a few shades darker than her fair skin.

"I'm thinking meatballs for dinner tonight," she says. "I'm going to hear Angela Davis speak at the public library."

There's a book by Angela Davis on the table and I open its pages.

When my dad comes home I find out he's going to hear Davis speak as well.

I don't mean to sigh dramatically, but I do.

"What was that sigh about?" he asks.

"Sometimes I feel like I missed out on all the interesting . . ." I am about to say *periods* but decide on *epochs* instead. My parents look at me quizzically. I probably didn't pronounce it right. I move on. "The Velvet Revolution in Czechoslovakia, and even here I missed Angela Davis, the Black Panthers, Patty Hearst . . ." I worry I sound like Gentle.

"Did I ever tell you about the time I saw Patty Hearst?" my dad says. He sits down in the study. This is going to be a story. I sit down across from him.

"I was walking one day on 30th Avenue. You were just a baby. I was going to the grocery store to get something for you. Diapers or a snack or toilet paper . . . What was it?" He looks at the floor.

"You can probably skip over that part," I say.

"Right," he says. "Anyway, I was going to the grocery store and I saw a Chevrolet parked on the street. There was a woman with glasses in the driver's seat, staring straight ahead. And then, in the back seat, behind what looked like dog-cage wire, there was a woman lying down across the seats. I thought, That's Patty Hearst.

"I continued walking to the store, got what I was buying, and then turned back home. By then the car was gone. I thought about it for a few hours and went over what I'd seen. The news said that she was in Pennsylvania at the time—that's what everyone thought—but I was convinced I'd seen her. The FBI was offering a $50,000 reward for any information about Patty Hearst, so that was tempting. But on the other hand, I was worried that the Symbionese Liberation Army would come after me, and I had a baby."

I point to myself. *Me?*

"Right. So, I thought about it for a few hours and then I called the hotline. The man I talked to didn't seem too interested in my story. Like I said, no one thought she was in San Francisco. But then, later, they found out she'd been in San Francisco all along. And when I saw the photos of the woman who was with her—the one with the glasses—I knew it was her. I knew I'd seen Patty Hearst."

"Wow," I say, genuinely impressed. "Where was it again?"

"30th and California."

"Right near Julia's house," I say. "I walk there every morning."

"Yeah, so if they had found her based on my call, I would be $50,000 richer, but on the other hand, I might be dead. And this house would be a tourist attraction. All the tour buses would go by and say, 'That's where they killed the man who revealed Patty Hearst's location.' So there you have it," he says.

I don't know what to say. "Thanks," I say.

"You're welcome," he says and stands. At the doorway to the study he pauses and turns back. "Oh, and Eulabee," he says, pretending he's had an afterthought. "I locked the liquor cabinet."

25

As I'm leaving school Tuesday afternoon I see a sign on the door to the front office. "Office closed this afternoon for emergency faculty meeting." I stand outside for a minute, contemplating the sign. Ms. Mc. and Ms. Catanese walk toward the front office with red envelopes in hand. I bend over and pretend to retie my shoelace, before moving on at a pace that is quick-while-trying-to-appear-slow.

I walk in the direction of my home. I see Keith on Lake Street with two friends I don't recognize. The three of them are on their skateboards. The two friends are wearing Thrasher sweatshirts. Keith's wearing one that says "Powell Peralta." As I approach, the friends stare at me. Keith looks away.

Shit, I think. They've heard about the blood.

"Hey Keith," I say. "How was Yosemite?"

His friends laugh. Keith doesn't answer.

I look down at the sidewalk, as though I can pretend it wasn't me who just spoke. I walk past them, with purpose and without looking back. When I'm out of their line of sight, I walk faster, though I'm unsure of my destination. The wind is strong today—all the better to dry the small pin-drops of water I feel collecting in the corners of my eyes.

I turn left on 25th Avenue, and now I know I'm headed to Baker Beach. I walk past a house where I used to babysit. One night the parents didn't come home when they said they would. The clock turned to ten, then slowly ticked its way to eleven. I called my parents. They asked if I knew where the couple had gone. I did not. I imagined car crashes. I imagined them dying and me having to break the news to the kids, whose lips were like rose petals and whose hair smelled of ketchup. Finally, at 12:37 a.m., the front door opened, and the parents spilled inside: scarves on the floor, their shoes thumping free, a hissed *Fuck!* directed at the corner of a rug that caused the mom to trip.

When I get down to the beach the sand whips in my face. The waves crash. High above me, on the cliffs, the homes aren't the sherbet-hued houses you find by other beaches in other towns. No, these houses are faded rusts and off-whites and mustard yellows, the colors of stains that don't come out in the wash.

I have an entire section of the beach to myself. The closest person to me is a man wrestling in the wind with his large fish-shaped kite. I walk toward the water. I decide I'll wait for the tide to greet me, the way an animal approaches its owner. When it recedes, I'll turn back toward home. I don't have far to walk—today the ocean extends higher up on the beach than usual. When I reach the wet sand, I hear a voice behind me.

"Bee!" it shouts.

I turn and see Keith, carrying his skateboard. I'm touched he's followed me, and I smile. But as he approaches me I see the furious expression on his face.

"So, is it true?" he says.

"Is what true?"

"You know," he says. He's out of breath from his strut across the sand.

"I don't know," I say. "Maybe you can be more specific."

"Okay," he says. "Did you, specifically, let Axel, specifically, fuck you at the party last weekend?"

"That's not what happened," I say. "We didn't . . . we didn't do it."

"Really?" he says. "That's not what I heard. I heard it was messy and there's proof."

"Keith," I say. The wind hits my face, and I feel myself get smaller. I feel like I'm one of those Russian stacking dolls that Madame Sonya has in the ballet studio—"Matryoshka," she calls them. All my outdoor layers are being taken away, revealing who I really am at my core is the smallest doll, the one with blurry features that can't stand on its own.

"We didn't have sex. It was a mistake. There was this bottle with alcohol. I thought it was a silver flask, but it was a shampoo bottle and . . ." Even describing the bottle makes my stomach tense and my throat gag. I lean forward, as though I'm about to vomit on the sand.

"Why would you do that?" Keith says. "Why would you even let him give you alcohol? That guy's a dick. You should hear the things he said about you."

We're near the sewer, and the wind lifts the stench to my nose and sand to my throat. Now I really do think I might vomit.

"Don't you have anything to say for yourself? Anything to say to me?"

I'm still curled over. I'm still the littlest Russian doll, on the verge of toppling. When I open my eyes and look up, Keith's gone. I turn and see him walking west, toward the bluff.

"Keith," I call out. "I'm sorry," I scream. But he doesn't turn around. I start to run toward him, while calling out his name. As I get closer, he sees me, and begins to run away from me. Now he's holding his skateboard like it's a baby he's protecting. He runs toward the promontory that separates Baker and China beaches. He'll have to stop when he gets to it. The tide is high, and there's no way to safely run around the bend. I slow down my pace, knowing this. He will stop and turn to me.

But I am mistaken. When he gets to the rocks, he doesn't stop. Instead, he starts to run around the bluff. I've done this dash a dozen times with Maria Fabiola, but only when the tide is low.

"Keith!" I call. "Stop!" I run to the water as an enormous wave whips against the rocks. "Keith!" I wait for a response. I stare at the ocean as though it will speak and that's when I see a shape in the water. It's a dark oblong object being tossed about as though on a trampoline. Keith's skateboard.

I watch the skateboard repeatedly crash against the rocks, swoop out to sea as the waves retract, and then smash against the rocks again. It's as though I'm watching a video installation on a continuous loop. For a moment time doesn't seem linear, but vertical.

I turn to look who's on the beach, who I can appeal to for help. But I am alone. The wind has driven everyone away. Even the kite flyer has left. This is a Northern California beach, so there are no lifeguards, no lifeguard towers. Where is Keith?

I know better than to run around the promontory— the tide is too high and I might suffer the same fate as . . . the same fate as the skateboard, I tell myself, finishing my thought differently than it began. I have no choice but to scale the rocks and see what I can from above. My hope is that Keith's safe on the other side of the bluff, that he's on China Beach. China Beach where I licked his webbed feet.

The rocks are slippery today. The waves have leapt unusually high, soaking every surface. I dig the pads of my fingers into any crevice I can find. It's more difficult for my sneakers to gain purchase. I slip down the cliff, my chin scraping against rock until I turn and offer the side of my head. I land hard on the sand. Pain reverberates in my skull. I wipe my chin, and my fingers bring blood to my lips. I spit. My lips are salty. Tears spring from my eyes, salting the cut.

I move inland and try the climb from a different approach. The bluff is higher from this starting point, but its face is jagged here, giving me more possibilities for traction. I start the ascent and soon am moving fast—hand, foot, hand, foot until I am at the top. I scurry to the edge. "Keith," I scream. I can barely hear myself against the roar of the waves. I try to peek down without falling. The skateboard is no longer visible.

I scramble down the other side of the cliff, to China Beach. First I slide, and then I turn so I'm facing the rocks. Foot, hand, foot, hand, until I push off and land on the sand. I turn and see a group of people maybe two hundred feet away.

The group is gathered around a bonfire. I run toward it, my eyes searching for Keith's tall frame. The smoke smudges my vision. The fire's smell is fierce. I cough, stop to catch my breath, and then resume my sprint.

As I approach the fire, I count nine people. None of them are Keith. It's a group of hippies and what look like homeless people, gathered around the flames, drinking. I stop running and walk toward them cautiously.

"Have you seen a boy?" I ask.

The face of a toothless man turns toward me. And then another face, this one of a woman with impossibly long hair, tilts in my direction. I address her. "Have you seen a boy?"

She is slow to speak, stoned out of her mind. "A boy?" she says. She turns to the others, their eyes all too wide or too small.

"A boy," they repeat to each other.

"I saw a boy this morning," a man in a beanie says, staring into the flames.

"He's tall. He would have been running by here," I say. "On the beach. Maybe ten minutes ago? Maybe five? Or twenty?" I have no idea how much time has passed.

"Have you seen a boy running by?" the long-haired woman asks the group. No one answers. Another woman starts singing a song that sounds Hawaiian.

"Offer our guest a drink," says the toothless man. He's addressing a young couple wearing wool ponchos. Between them they gingerly pass a bottle of booze.

"I don't want a drink," I say. "I'm trying to find a friend."

"I'll be your friend," says a voice by the fire. It's the voice of an old woman with hair short and straight, like a monk's. She turns her head toward me. Her eyes are so blank that at first I mistake them for blind.

"I was asking if anyone saw my friend," I say.

"I saw a boy," she says. "He was running."

"Where?" I say.

She points to the ocean.

"There," she says. "He was running into the ocean."

"Into the ocean?" I say. *Fucking hippies!* She's now been passed a large bong and she places it on the sand in front of her and hunches over it as though it's a microscope. She's forgotten my existence.

The toothless man moves toward me, his unshowered stench so pungent the smoke isn't strong enough to disguise it. I step away and to the side, avoiding him. In the distance, descending the steps to the sand, I see two policemen. I gather my strength and run toward them.

"Hey, where are you going?" I hear a voice call out from behind me. "Why leave the party?"

The cops see me running toward them, and in response, they run to meet me. Their gait is slow—they're weighed down by their belts and batons, and now that they're on the beach, they struggle with the sand.

"Are you here because of Keith?" I say. "Did you find him?"

"Who?" one asks.

"There's a boy," I explain.

"Is he with the bonfire?" the other cop asks. "We're here to put out the bonfire."

"No," I say. And I tell them about Keith, about how he tried to run around the cliff. I tell them everything

I know. One of the officers uses his CB radio, as the other sprints toward the cliff. Then the cop with the radio turns to me. "Are you okay?" he asks.

"Yes," I say. I realize he's looking at the side of my head. "I'm just worried about my friend."

"Okay, we'll find him," he says. "Backup and an ambulance are on their way. I think I have all the information I need from you, but we need to make sure you get warm."

"I'll be fine," I say.

"I'll be back," the cop says. Then he runs past the bonfire.

I turn and start walking toward the steps. I have to leave. They'll find him. They'll find his body? They'll find his body in the angry ocean.

26

At the top of the ninety-three steps I sit against the sign that cautions, in multiple languages, that people have been swept from the beach to their deaths. My body feels robbed of muscle and bone. I run my fingers through my hair and find it's wet. I stare at my hand: blood. I push my hair back and pull up the hood of my sweatshirt. I stare at my legs and my arms, which are badly, wildly scraped. The crosshatching red lines are intriguing—they go in all directions, like the markings left by a glacier.

I remember I have sweatpants in my backpack. I pull them up over my legs. I remove my blue uniform skirt and stuff it deep into my backpack. Then I stand to walk. But where?

I don't want to go home. I can't go home. I have led a boy to his death. Could that phrase be applied here? I did lead him *to* the beach, but then he ran *from* me to his death. The accurate charge is that I led a boy to *run to* his death. I can't tell my parents. I can't tell anyone.

My head feels better when cradled inside the sweatshirt hood, so I walk with one hand holding the hood in place. I walk and walk until I find myself on Clement Street. The curtains of the ballet school are closed. The upstairs window is shut. I don't know where Madame Sonya is but I'm relieved she's not home. I turn into the passageway on the right of the building, step over the hose that's lying on the ground like a noose, and I line up the stubborn numbers on the padlock to 1938. The sound of the lock opening is the sound of freedom.

I enter the shed, close the door behind me, and lie down on the pink divan. Where is the furry white blanket, I wonder? And then I recall the news reports. Maria Fabiola was found on Christmas Day on her parents' doorstep, wrapped in a blanket like a newborn.

Yellow light drapes over me like mosquito netting. I dream that the long-haired woman from the beach hands me what I think is a flower, but when she opens her palm it grows into a bowler hat. She places it on my head and it's too tight.

I **wake** with my hands over my ears. My head feels like a Cubist painting. The hair on one side of my head—the side I offered to the rocks to save my face—is sticky with a viscous substance.

I search for a mirror in the shed. But there's no mirror, no reflective surface, not even in the small bathroom. This is a space built to resist, and even repel, the passing of time. On the walls hang dried bouquets, retired pointe shoes, and *The Raft of the Medusa*. I crack open the door and see that it's grown lighter outside. How is that possible? And then I check my watch. It's seven. In the morning. I have slept through the night. Or two nights. What day is it?

And then I remember Keith. I wonder if the cops found his body, if the ambulance took him to the hospital. I wonder if, when hearing the ambulances' sirens, cars pulled to the right of the streets or if they ignored the wails.

If I go home, I will be in trouble for staying out for the night, or two nights. And in more serious, life-haunting trouble because of Keith. There will be many, many questions. I will be hated, more hated than I already am.

If I stay away for a little longer, I can recover. I can nurse myself back to health and make a plan. I can figure out what to say about Keith, how to explain what happened.

I step outside the shed and tiptoe down the passageway and out onto Clement Street. The street is unpopulated except for a Chinese grocer opening his corner shop and two elderly women speaking Russian while they wait for their tiny dogs to finish sniffing each other.

I enter the small corner store. I need aspirin. And breakfast food. In a shopping basket I collect a bottle of orange juice, a box of Cheerios, and aspirin and approach the cash register.

"Is your head okay?" the grocer asks.

The hood of my sweatshirt has slid off. I hastily pull it back on.

The plastic bag crinkles loudly as I scamper back to the shed. Once inside, I secure the door behind me and sit down on the rug. I tear open the Cheerios so hastily I don't realize the box is upside down. I scoop out handfuls of cereal and eat. The chewing sounds too loud. The chewing hurts my head. I open the bottle of orange juice and drink a quarter of it in one long gulp. I remember the aspirin. It's difficult for me to twist off the kid-proof top. I take three pills and wash them down with more juice.

I force myself to scoot back onto the divan where surely it will be more comfortable. This act of moving requires ridiculous effort. I sit cross-legged and give myself instructions. "Think!" I say aloud. My voice sounds gravelly, surprising. I place my hands on either side of my face, as though I can force my head to look in the direction of the future.

I force myself to think but no thoughts appear. I picture thought bubbles in cartoons. The ones above my head are empty. I wake from a nap on the divan and spot an autumnally red leaf, the size of a quarter, where my head was resting. I try to pick it up and realize it's dried blood.

I need to find a newspaper, to see if there's news about Keith. I sneak out of the shed, in case Madame Sonya is home, and out onto Clement Street. I see a yellow newspaper box and approach it cautiously, afraid of what the headline might be. But the front page has nothing about Keith. The main article is about tax reform. I insert my coins and take out a copy and bring it into the shed. I sit on the floor and skim every section, every page. Not a single mention of Keith. Nothing.

27

In the early afternoon I go out for food again, and I see a face I recognize. It's my cousin Lazlo standing near the theater across the street. He's holding hands with a man who's clearly older than he is. Lazlo is eighteen. I look up at the marquee of the small art-house theater: *My Beautiful Laundrette* is playing. There's a matinee showing.

"Eula?" Lazlo says to me, and quickly drops the hand of his companion.

I haven't seen Lazlo for three years. We used to be close before my father and Lazlo's mom had a falling out. That's what my dad calls it, a falling out. My mother calls it a travesty.

"You okay?" Lazlo says. "What happened to your head?"

"I guess I fell," I say, indicating the top of my ear. It hurts to touch the wound directly.

"You *guess* you fell?" he says.

"Yeah," I say. He's still a teenager, but he has a thin mustache that wasn't there last time I saw him. His hair is dark blond, his cheeks round, his eyes set deep in his face. We could be mistaken for siblings.

"Maybe I should take you back to your house," he says.

"You drive?" I say.

"Yeah," he says, hesitantly.

"You have a car?" I say.

"My friend does," he says, and then looks around. The man whose hand he was holding has vanished. "Joel?" Lazlo calls out.

"Where'd he go?" I ask.

"Probably back to his wife and kids," Lazlo says. He tries to disguise the anger in his voice but that only makes him sound angrier.

"Stay here a second," he says.

"Okay," I say reluctantly, as though waiting is an inconvenience. I like pretending I have someplace to be. I watch Lazlo run down the block and come back, and then run in the other direction. His torso seems unusually long, his legs small and rubbery like a centipede's. "Joel!" he calls out. "Joel?" His dark blue Members Only jacket inflates as it gathers wind.

When he returns he looks distracted and defeated.

"Should I walk you home?" he says.

"I can't go home," I say.

"I've been in that situation," he says.

But have you led a boy to his death? I want to ask.

Instead I say: "I've missed you."

We end up taking two buses to his house, which used to be my grandma's house before she died. Now a small herd of my Hungarian relatives live there—Lazlo, his mother, Ágota (my aunt), his sister Jazmin, and another cousin, Zsolt, and his family. I'm not sure how cousin Zsolt is related to me, and there's some question in my family about whether or not he is in fact related to us. But he's a contractor or carpenter, and helps keep the house intact.

"Will everyone be there?" I say. We're sitting side by side on the slippery orange seats of the bus.

"I don't know," Lazlo says. "Some people are working. Jazmin's knocked up," he says.

My cousin Jazmin is twenty.

"Who was the old man outside the theater?"

"He's not that old."

"He was at least forty."

"He's thirty-four." Lazlo grows somber. "I know him from this restaurant where I work. He's confused."

"You kiss him?" I ask.

"I'm not answering that," he says.

"Does your mom know you're gay?"

"I haven't told her anything but I think she knows," he says, and rests his head on the seat in front of us. "She's always making comments about Harvey Milk," he says to the floor of the bus.

"My dad met Mayor Feinstein once," I say. "He said she had nice calves."

Lazlo sits up straight and looks at me like I'm an idiot.

Lazlo's mom, Ágota, and my dad had a falling out over the kinds of things siblings usually have falling outs over: money and love. My father made money and Aunt Ágota lost money. Then there was some disagreement about how their mother, my grandmother, should live. My father thought a retirement home. Ágota wanted to be paid to take care of her. The argument didn't help anyone. In the end my grandmother died anyway.

Then all my relatives who couldn't afford their own places moved into my grandma's house, which wasn't big to begin with. I've just heard this from Lazlo. I haven't been to the house since my grandmother passed.

We get off the bus in West Portal, and walk a few blocks through the sleepy residential neighborhood and into her small, gray house. It's strange how many things are still the same from when my grandma was alive and living there—the clock radio by the yellow refrigerator, all the miniature ceramic dogs she collected.

From the kitchen I can look down into the rectangular garden and see that Jazmin is asleep by the apple tree. From this angle she looks so natural, like an earth mother relaxing in the garden on a sunny but crisp winter day. But Jazmin is no earth mother. Her nails have always been long and fake, her clothes black.

"You want to go say hi?" Lazlo asks.

"Nah," I say. "I think she should sleep. I mean, she's pregnant."

"Yeah," he says.

We both watch Jazmin for a moment, and I'm surprised she doesn't wake from our collective stares.

"I'm not really sure what I'm doing here," I say.

We play Centipede and Pac-Man. Eventually Jazmin comes inside.

"What the . . . ?" she says when she sees me but doesn't give me a hug. I congratulate her on her pregnancy. She shrugs. Her small green eyes look even smaller now that she's gained weight, and maybe it's the pregnancy but her dark-blond bob looks much thicker than it used to be. The phone rings and she goes to answer it in the other room. Her gait is colt-like even though her stomach is huge. After a few minutes she comes back and looks at me strangely and for a second too long. "Let's get that head of yours cleaned up, Eulabee," she says.

I follow her into the bathroom. When she opens the medicine cabinet above the sink, I feel a sinking sadness in my chest. My grandma's pink Oil of Olay moisturizer and her Pond's cold cream are still sitting on the bottom shelf. I know the way these creams smell, and how they made my grandma's face shiny and cool when I kissed her goodnight on the evenings I stayed over at her house.

Jazmin takes some tissue paper and wets it and aggressively pats the side of my head. "Ow," I say.

"I'm just trying to get it clean," she says.

The wet towel makes the blood run more; a thin pink stream trickles down my face. Jazmin takes out an Ace bandage from the cabinet and tries to wrap it around my head. Her long nails repeatedly poke me.

"It really hurts," I say when she fastens the Ace bandage. I start to unravel it.

"Fine," she says, not sounding like it's fine. She leaves the bathroom and I finish removing the bandage. It's now stained with blood and ruined but I roll it up and put it in the medicine cabinet anyway. Then I remove the Oil of Olay and apply it to my face with small circular motions the way my grandma taught me.

When I come out of the bathroom Lazlo is sitting in the den shuffling a deck of cards and I sit down across from him. Just when he finishes dealing, I hear people climbing the stairs. Zsolt, the builder who's supposedly related to me, enters the room. He's in his late twenties and wearing a shiny suit. His wife, Eileen, walks up the stairs behind him wearing a dress with shoulder pads. She has a vast mane of black hair that climbs precariously high from her forehead. Her blouse is missing a button so I can see her beige bra. She makes a big production of hugging me. She's wearing my grandmother's rings.

Neither of them seems very surprised to see me at the house and I deduce that Jazmin told them on the phone. No one asks why I'm not at school that day. While Eileen makes dinner—I can smell the cabbage cooking—Zsolt comes into the den and turns on the TV to watch the news. He sits in the reclining chair where my grandfather used to sit.

The volume is too low for me to hear what the anchorwoman is saying, but I see the headline flash across the screen: "Another Missing Child Case in Sea Cliff."

They must not have found Keith. I blink hard. Then I see a familiar face on the screen. It's me. My photo from last year's school yearbook is on TV. In the photo, I'm standing in front of the bush at Spragg where the butterflies gather. It takes me a minute to make sense of what the news is saying: it's me who's missing, not Keith. I am missing. And then the segment is over and I'm followed by a pile-up on a freeway.

"Eulabee," Zsolt says.

I turn to him but can't speak. It seems too soon to be missing on TV.

Lazlo turns to me. "You have to call your parents."

"Okay," I say. "Where's the phone?"

I follow Lazlo into the kitchen, where Zsolt and Eileen are setting the table. The phone is on the wall by the bread box. I pick up the receiver.

"What are you doing?" Eileen says, alarmed, like I've picked up a gun.

"She needs to call home," Lazlo says.

"No," Zsolt's wife finally says. "We're still on that phone plan your grandma had. We only get three calls a month."

I remember the system. When I would call my parents from my grandma's house, I'd let the phone ring twice and then hang up. That was the signal to my parents to call me back. I consider doing that now—dialing their number and letting it ring twice so they know to call. But they won't be expecting me to be calling from my grandma's house.

Lazlo reads my mind. "Can't she use it this once?" he says.

"Let your dad sweat a little," says Zsolt. "What has he given us? Let him get us a better phone plan. He can afford it."

"This is crazy," Lazlo says. "Eulabee's on TV. Joe and Greta think she's dead or kidnapped."

"She's fine," Eileen says. "I'll call them later."

"But the cops?" Lazlo said. "They're looking for her."

"Fuck the cops!" Zsolt scoffs.

Eileen places bowls of cabbage soup on the place mats. The table is too big for the small room and there are too many chairs. There's no room to move.

"Sit down, Eulabee," Zsolt says, gesturing at the last chair.

I can't get out of the house fast enough. I run down the stairs, and down the street. The bus comes right away, like it's been waiting to take me home.

28

I get off the second bus at 25th Avenue and as I approach my house I see two news vans. The lights in my house appear to be off, but I'm sure my parents are home. An anchorwoman is standing in front of a palm tree giving a live report. I turn around and run without stopping until I get to the ballet school.

I open the door to the shed and find a figure sitting on the couch. I scream.

"Well done," Maria Fabiola says. "I never knew you wanted to be in the spotlight."

Seeing another person in the shed seems like a terrible invasion. Maria Fabiola appears outsized, like a fairy-tale wolf.

"What?" I say, closing the door behind me. "You're totally wrong."

"Um, then why are you hiding in this shed?" Maria Fabiola says. She gestures around the room, as though to remind me of my environment.

"I did something bad," I say.

"Yeah, everyone knows that you wrote the valentines," Maria Fabiola says. "There aren't that many clever girls in our class who are also that stupid. And when you didn't show up for school it was obvious it was you."

"That's not the reason I didn't show up," I say. "I didn't come to school because I hit my head on the rocks when I was trying to save Keith."

"Save Keith?" Maria Fabiola says. "Why does he need saving?"

"We were at Baker the other day and it was high tide and he tried to run around to China Beach, but . . ."

"But what?" She's looking at me with mouth agape.

"I don't think he made it," I whisper dramatically.

"You don't think he made it?" Maria Fabiola says. She sits upright. "Eulabee!" she says and starts laughing. "I just saw Keith on my way over here. Like twenty minutes ago!"

"What? Where?"

"He was at the park with his usual crew. Lance and White Charlie."

"Oh my god," I say. "Oh my god." I want to collapse with relief on the couch next to her but when she sees me approaching, she doesn't move to make space. Instead I lie down on the furry rug.

"That's why you're here?" she says. "Because you thought Keith was dead? I hope if you ever think *I'm* dead you don't go into hiding. I figured you were here because of the valentines. The teachers are fucking *pissed*. Everyone's assuming you'll be expelled. Just for the '*I miss your boobs*' one alone. And *Sexo*? You can do better."

I can't think. I want to ask about Julia but decide it hardly matters.

"But listen," Maria Fabiola says. "I have a plan. You know how I'm supposed to be on ABC? You know how I did the B-roll?"

Again with the B-roll.

"The truth is that they asked a bunch of questions and I didn't always get the story right," she says. "Or I guess there were inconsistencies. So they said they were 'doing some research' and would get back to me. And meanwhile Mr. Makepeace is acting weird toward me now. So I had an idea."

"But first will you please admit you made up that story?"

"I didn't make it up," she says. She says this with enough conviction that I know everyone but me would believe her. She is good.

"You borrowed it from a book," I say.

She's weighing her options. She takes off half her bracelets from one wrist and transfers them to the other. "I got the rough outline from *Treasure Island*. But I came up with lots of new details. Good ones."

"*Kidnapped*," I say. "Not *Treasure Island*."

"Okay. Good for you," she says. "You're wonderful."

I actually do feel wonderful. Because I guess her idea.

"You want me to say I was kidnapped, too."

"It helps us both," she says, now in a school-counselor voice. "It *saves* us both."

"Kidnapped by the same people?" I ask. "Who was it again? Pirates? Actual pirates?"

"We can change that," she says. "As long as the stories are similar. I'll say they gave me Stockholm syndrome and you can say you already had it, being Swedish and all."

I don't know where to start. She is not bright enough to pull this off.

"Otherwise, Eulabee, you're expelled," she says.

Or maybe she is.

"You'll never get into any high school if you've been expelled, but you'll get into any high school—every high school—if you've been *kidnapped*."

I know she's right. Maria Fabiola scoots over to make room for me on the couch. "So what are your thoughts?" she asks.

"I thought *you* had a plan," I say.

"I do, but I want to hear yours first."

Of course she has no plan.

"I do think it should be maybe more logical kidnappers this time," she says.

There is no way this will work with her. She is the worst possible partner for a scheme like this.

"I was thinking the Mob could be involved," she says.

"No," I say. "Let's back up a second."

"What about Melvin Belli, the lawyer?" she says.

I haven't heard of Melvin Belli. "Listen," I say. "It has to be realistic. You said that yourself. Let's think of an actual situation that might have happened."

"The guy in the white car!" she says, lighting up. I realize it's a relatively brilliant idea. But it would mean I was lying about him when it first happened, or didn't happen. I decide I can't lie *now* about telling the truth *then*.

"No. Too complicated," I say, and the light inside Maria Fabiola goes out. "We need a name," I say. "We need something big, to erase the other stories and lies. We need a headline."

"What about Neal Cassady?" she says. "Maybe he drugged us and made us marry him. He's a polygamist."

"I think he's dead," I tell her. "How about Jerry Garcia drugged us?"

She likes this. "Then he made us clean his guitars!"

"And tie-dye his shirts," I say.

"And we have some dirt on him, like he's secretly really into football."

I'm ready to settle on Jerry Garcia but then realize at the time of our kidnapping he was probably playing a six-hour show at a stadium somewhere in Ohio.

"We need someone whose exact whereabouts are not known on a day-to-day basis," I say.

"They never found the Zodiac Killer," she says. "Maybe he kidnapped us and made us research astrological signs."

Suddenly I feel overwhelmed by everything ahead of me. I slip myself off the couch and onto the rug again.

"Don't worry," she says, and lowers herself off the couch so she's seated next to me. "I've got this figured out. You come back. We present our stories so they're parallel. They add up, and we have a big name for the kidnapper. Then we both go on ABC. You'll have to do B-roll, too, since I already did mine. B-roll is really fun. You walk up and down the sidewalk, open doors, pretend to do your homework. You can wear that pretty polka-dot dress."

"I don't know," I say.

"You're tired," she says like she's my babysitter. "Let me take you back to your parents and make sure you're okay. We'll figure out everything there." She stands and offers me her hand to help me up. "Don't worry," she says. "I won't let you out of my sight."

She and I leave the shed and start making our way back to Sea Cliff together. As we pass the park, I spot Keith from half a block away. He has a new skateboard. When he sees me, he looks down.

"He's ignoring me," I say.

"No, he's not," Maria Fabiola says. "That's the look of someone who's deeply ashamed."

I watch him and think Maria Fabiola might be right.

When we approach my house we're careful to go in through the alleyway to avoid the news vans. The back door is locked even though my parents are home, so I get the spare key from the hiding place.

"Wait," Maria Fabiola says as we step into the kitchen. "We should do a big reveal."

"Who's there?" Svea calls out from another room.

"It's just Maria Fabiola," she says. "Go get your parents."

A minute later, the door to the kitchen swings open and my mom and dad enter the room.

"Surprise!" Maria Fabiola yells.

There are hugs and sobs—Maria Fabiola does most of the dramatic sobbing. I hug Svea extra-tight. My parents want to know where I've been and I tell them the short version, that I hurt my head, that I was at Grandma's house.

"Yes, we know that part," my dad says. "Lazlo called us a few hours ago and said you were on your way home."

I'm surprised and touched that Lazlo called them. I'm also grateful because it clearly saved my parents worry. They don't seem as upset with me as I feared. Or more likely, I realize, they're being kind now because they're relieved I'm safe. But within twenty-four hours I'll be grounded till college.

My mother checks my head. "It's a surface wound," she proudly pronounces.

Svea serves us tea. She places doilies under our cups.

My father asks me if anything strange happened. "No," I tell him. My mother asks how my relatives are. "The same," I tell her.

"What can we do for you?" my father asks. "What do you need?"

"I really want everything to go back to normal as quickly as possible," I say. "I want normal again."

"Of course you do. I totally understand," Maria Fabiola says performatively and leans over to give me an awkward hug. In my ear she whispers, "Good job."

The three of them stare at me and Maria Fabiola, like they can't really believe we're there.

"Are you hungry?" my dad says and gets up.

"We're *famished*!" Maria Fabiola says. I've never heard her say this word before, and I'm not at all hungry, but decide that anything that restores routine is good, so I say I'm hungry, too. Maria Fabiola calls her mom and asks if she can stay with me tonight. "To help Eulabee reacclimate," she says to her mother.

I look around the study. I've only been gone a day but everything looks new to me. I examine the dolls from around the world that I collected when I was younger. A doll in a red flamenco dress. A doll wearing a kimono. I used to think they were collector's items but now they look tacky. Their dresses are made of poor material, their facial expressions a bizarre mixture of boredom and astonishment.

"I'm assuming you're going to school tomorrow, Maria Fabiola?" my mom says. "Do you want me to wash your uniform tonight?"

"Absolutely I'm going," Maria Fabiola says. "I think we should both go. I mean, Eulabee was saying she wanted everything to go back to normal quickly. And we should probably let everyone at school know she's okay so they stop worrying. I heard rumors of a vigil being planned."

My mother looks at me. "I want to go," I say.

"Well, your father already called the detectives," my mom says. "But I'll call Mr. Makepeace tomorrow morning."

Dinner is quiet but for Maria Fabiola's frequent yawns, which are all demonstrably fake. She's setting us up for a quick after-dinner departure.

"Well, we're exhausted!" she says, and squeezes my knee under the table. "Do you mind if we don't help clean up?"

"You don't have to," my mother says. I realize that Maria Fabiola holds a spell over my family just as she does over her friends. I suspect I'm not getting in as much trouble as I deserve because she's here.

Ewa is spending a few days with another au pair, so Maria Fabiola will sleep in Ewa's bed in the room next to mine. I get into bed and instantly my eyes are leaden. Maria Fabiola's room is between mine and the hallway. She's standing in the doorway, a prison guard in a Lanz nightgown.

"Sleep now," she says, "and tomorrow we'll polish our stories on the way to school. Then at lunch I'll use the office phone to call ABC and tell them we can talk to them together. Eulabee?"

I'm already nodding off. "What?" I mumble.

"I'm so glad it was you who was kidnapped," she says.

I don't know what to say to that. Sleep is dissolving me.

"I was thinking of saying that to ABC," she says, as she stands high above me. "'I'm so glad it was you.' What do you think?"

29

I wake up to Maria Fabiola's stomach. She's standing by my bed, shaking my shoulder. "Good, you're finally awake. Your parents wanted to let you sleep in, but we have to leave for school. We've got fifteen minutes."

I close my eyes.

"No, no, don't go back to sleep," she says. "Your mom talked to Mr. Makepeace. He's going to welcome you back at assembly. Then he wants to talk to us at morning recess. Then the *Chronicle* wants to do a joint interview this afternoon. We have a full day, Sunshine."

I can't believe this person, the multitudes she contains.

"What are we going to say?" I ask.

"We'll get our stories straight on the walk," she says. "The *Chronicle* will be good practice for ABC. I'll have to call the producer and let them know that because they took their sweet time, the *Chronicle* is now interested. That'll get them motivated!" She lays my uniform on the bed.

"But just get dressed fast," she says. As I sit up I see my mother has not only washed but pressed Maria Fabiola's middy and blue skirt—I can smell the scent of an iron wafting from her uniform. We usually wear our socks to our ankles, but now Maria Fabiola's wearing them pulled up almost to her knees, and with a pair of my loafers that I rarely wear.

She turns her back to me and rummages through the change drawer of my desk. "Don't tell me you're putting pennies in the loafers," I say.

"Just get dressed," she says. "We're in a hurry."

We're about to walk out the door when my dad calls out to us. "No, no, no," he says. "I'll drive you girls."

"That's okay, Joe," Maria Fabiola says. She calls my parents by their first names and they somehow go along with it.

"We can walk," I say.

"Not a chance," he says. "I'm driving you."

In the car we have no time to coordinate our stories. My mom is in the passenger seat, and Svea is sitting in the back between us. Maria Fabiola tries to write me a note but her handwriting is a disaster, and besides, it's only a two-minute drive. When we get to school we're surrounded.

At the morning assembly my parents sit to my right in the front row and Maria Fabiola sits to my left, massaging my hand. Mr. Makepeace wears a red bow tie. When he makes an announcement welcoming me back, the applause is thunderous.

My parents depart after the assembly to talk with Mr. Makepeace and Ms. Catanese in the front office. Maria Fabiola and Julia flank me as we walk through campus, while Faith follows behind us like a lady in waiting. I'm thrilled by the sudden re-embracement of my former friends and all my classmates—the incessant hugs, the earnest welcome-back letters (a few mangled flowers) slipped through the slots of my locker.

Our first class after the assembly is English. Mr. London announces that we're starting a new unit on Homer's *Odyssey*. I know that this is another ruse to impress high schools and parents. No other kids our age are reading *The Odyssey* but that is the point of Spragg.

Mr. London has purchased new chalk. "HOME," he writes on the board in big, messy writing. We're taught to write neatly and within the lines, but we've also been taught that all men with sloppy handwriting are brilliant.

"What does *home* mean to you?" he says, his hands behind his back.

He looks at the front row.

"Food?" says Tua, a famously anorexic girl.

"Okay," Mr. London says, and writes "food" on the chalkboard, and then adds "nourishment" beneath it.

"What else?"

"Annoying sisters," says K.T., who is alone in thinking she's the class clown. She shrugs and looks around the class as though to say *Am I right?* Everyone stares mournfully at their erasers.

Mr. London dutifully records her response in messy writing. He blows on the chalk. "Maria Fabiola?" he says.

"Home is refuge after a long journey," she says.

He nods at her, sympathetically. "Refuge," he says, and writes it on the board. He underlines the word three times.

I know it won't be long before he calls on me. He will say my name as though it's an afterthought, when in fact I know his entire lesson is geared to me and Maria Fabiola, the girls who disappeared and came back.

"Eulabee?" he says.

"Doilies," I say.

"Right," he says. "Good." But he doesn't write *doilies* on the board.

We have our next class apart—we're in different sections of math. Maria Fabiola and I have arranged to meet after class in the hallway so we can walk to Mr. Makepeace's office together and make a plan. I wait for her until I'm about to be late, and wonder if there was a mix-up on my part. I rush to the office and say hello to Ms. Patel, the secretary, and take a seat. While I'm waiting, I pick up a pamphlet titled "Financial Aid at Spragg." On the cover is a photo of a biracial girl from seventh grade. Everyone knows she's from one of the wealthiest families in the school—her father is a well-known musician. They pay full tuition and are big donors to the annual school raffle.

As soon as Maria Fabiola walks in I see the reason for why she's late: she's somehow put her hair in two French braids that intertwine just above the nape of her neck. It makes her look at once more vulnerable and more formidable. She sits down next to me. "Zodiac Killer wannabe," she says. "That's the story."

Mr. Makepeace and Ms. Catanese come out of his office with a slender woman in a pink cardigan and tight black pants. She has thin skin that reveals wrinkles sprouting from her mouth and her nose, but still she's luminous, the kind of woman who might live on Nob Hill with Siamese cats and a lover.

"Girls," Mr. Makepeace says, "we're going to have to change the order of events here. I was hoping to meet with you before the *Chronicle* interview so I could hear more about the terrible, terrible experience you've endured, but it appears that our journalist had to come a little ahead of schedule—ahead of the detectives, even! I'd like to introduce you to my friend Shelley Shein—"

"Stine," the journalist interrupts. "Shelley Stine."

Mr. Makepeace blushes furiously. "Yes, my friend Shelley Stine. She'll take good care of you . . ." His error with the journalist's name has robbed him of linguistic certainty. "You young women," he finally says.

We introduce ourselves and shake her hand, which is oddly calloused. Then we're led to a small conference room, where Maria Fabiola and I are seated side by side in swivel chairs. Shelley Stine's beauty seems to have a hypnotic effect on Mr. Makepeace and Ms. Catanese—the second Shelley Stine asks them to leave so she can speak to us privately, they retreat, scuttling backward like crabs.

"Oh it goes without saying you should feel free to ask them about their history here," Mr. Makepeace adds from the doorway. "They've both attended Spragg since kindergarten and are exemplary students."

"Wonderful," Shelley Stine says and gives him a smile that's meant to simultaneously win him over and hasten his exit.

She turns to us with a different smile, the smile of a confidante. "So I should be honest with you girls since I expect you to be honest with me. For years I've been covering gardening for the paper. And women's issues. But no one else, well, was disposed to doing this piece right now. Plus it's winter and flowers aren't exactly blooming, so I stepped up for the job."

"No one else was disposed because ABC might still do something, right?" Maria Fabiola says.

"Sure," Shelley Stine says. "That's one explanation."

"Even though they don't have an exclusive anymore, I'll have to call ABC to let them know I talked to you. But our story will still be on the front page, right?" Maria Fabiola says. "Above the fold?"

"I really can't promise you where it'll be placed," Shelley Stine says, "but let's get started, shall we?" She peers at the first question in her notebook. "How do you girls like school?"

"We like it," I say. "It's a good school."

Maria Fabiola stares at me.

"The school has quite a reputation," Shelley Stine says. "Shakespeare in fifth grade, Goethe in seventh. And I understand now you're reading Homer?"

Amazing, I think. Mr. London's already gotten to her.

"So my question is," she continues. "Do you ever feel the academic pressure is too intense?"

"Not really," I say.

Shelley Stine doesn't bother to write down anything I've said.

"And what about you, Maria Fabiola?" Shelley Stine asks. "What do you think about the academic load?"

"Well, I've been coming here since kindergarten. Even then, our valentines were critiqued."

I look at Maria Fabiola—why is she bringing up valentines?

"Oh," says Shelley Stine, waiting for more. We are silent. "So," she continues, "the school has a reputation for being a pressure cooker. Do you ever get a break?"

"Sure," Maria Fabiola says. "We have a week at the end of the school year when we get to study something else besides the usual curriculum."

"What does that mean?" Shelley Stine asks.

"Well, sewing, for example," Maria Fabiola says.

"Sewing," Shelley Stine repeats. "Interesting." She sits more upright. "What else?"

It's my chance, I think. I know what catnip is for Shelley Stine and, not wanting to be outdone by Maria Fabiola, I offer it now. "There's also a class about how to look good in a bathing suit."

Shelley Stine not only swivels her chair in my direction, but scoots it toward me.

"Can you elaborate?" she says, her pen upright and bouncing on the pad of paper like a marathon runner waiting for the gun to go off.

"I can," Maria Fabiola says, and Shelley Stine swivels her chair back toward her. "We have this class called Bathing Suits Your Body."

"Excuse me," Shelley Stine says. "Bathing Suits . . ."

"It's a pun," I add, "like bathing *suits* your body."

She scribbles. "Puns. Good," she says.

"Anyway," Maria Fabiola says loudly, bringing the focus back to her. "In the class, we have to weigh in at the beginning of the week and then at the end of the week. The point is to look good in bathing suits."

"Bikinis or one pieces?" Shelley Stine asks.

"Well, it wasn't really specified," Maria Fabiola says, and seems momentarily puzzled by this oversight. "But the point is to look better at the end of the week than you do at the start. We weighed ourselves at the start of the week and the numbers were written down on our instructor's clipboard. Then we spent our days doing jumping jacks, running to the beach, and biking to a hostel in the Marin Headlands where we spent the night. At the hostel we were only allowed to eat salad while all the other kids around us had hamburgers and s'mores."

"That's all you were allowed?"

"Well, the instructors packed the food, right? And they just packed salad for us. They had steaks for themselves."

"Weren't you hungry?" Shelley Stine asks.

"So hungry!" Maria Fabiola roars. "But the whole bike ride to the hostel, they were telling us our bike seats were close to grazing our back tires! So that kind of made us feel bad about eating."

"Who were the teachers?"

"They all happened to be male," Maria Fabiola says. "Not Mr. Makepeace, but all the other male teachers. Every one."

"I can't believe it!" Shelley Stine says, seeming desperate to believe it. "Why weren't there any female teachers?"

"They all stayed home with their families, I guess," Maria Fabiola says.

This is not true. Ms. Livesey was on the trip with us.

"What happened at the end of the week?" Shelley Stine asks. Her pen can barely keep up with Maria Fabiola.

"Well, I mentioned that we had to get on the scale at the start of the week, right?"

Shelley Stine nods. "Yes, but I want to be clear—it was men who weighed you?"

"Yes," Maria Fabiola says. "Then they weighed us at the end of the week. And the differences in our weight from the start to the end of the course were tabulated."

"Like grades," Shelley Stine says.

"Exactly," Maria Fabiola says.

"You say it," Shelley Stine suggests.

"Like grades," Maria Fabiola says, and Shelley Stine writes this quote down.

I'm listening to everything Maria Fabiola is saying and I realize it's almost accurate, and yet it sounds so different when she tells it than what we experienced. The truth was that Maria Fabiola and I ranked the Bathing Suits Your Body class as our first choice. We were the ones who wanted to lose a few pounds so that we could impress Madame Sonya. We were the ones who wanted to get in better shape for climbing the cliffs at China Beach. We wanted to spend time with Ms. Livesey because she painted at night and her son was cute. With profound clarity I realize now that Maria Fabiola has talents I will never have.

"Just checking to make sure everything's going okay in here," Mr. Makepeace says, sticking his head through the door.

"It's just great!" Shelley Stine says, her smile incandescent.

"Happy to hear it," he says.

No, you won't be, I think.

Mr. Makepeace gives her the thumbs-up sign and closes the door. Shelley Stine's mouth drops into a frown.

"Okay. Now I have to get into the hard part. I don't want to re-traumatize you, but of course our readers will be interested in your disappearances."

"Kidnappings," Maria Fabiola corrects her.

"Okay," she says. "Tell me what happened first."

"It was a Thursday," Maria Fabiola says.

"I thought it was a Wednesday," Shelley Stine says. "December 12 was a Wednesday."

"Oh right," Maria Fabiola says. "I was thinking of Eulabee."

"But she went missing on a Tuesday," Shelley Stine says.

"Well . . ." Maria Fabiola says, and her eyes are suddenly wet. I'm certain she's willed them to be. I am in awe. "The kidnappings were very traumatic for both of us. And the kidnapper had a thing about trying to confuse us about our dates. The place where he kept us was full of calendars, and all of them were different. Like from different years."

"Can you elaborate on that, please?" Shelley Stine says.

Maria Fabiola nods with her whole body. "I can, Shelley. I think the kidnapper wanted to be the Zodiac Killer—he was like a Zodiac copycat—so he was very into horoscopes as you can imagine."

Shelley Stine pauses for a moment. "Yes, I can imagine. Please go on."

She writes something down, underlines it, and quickly flips the page of her notebook.

"Well, he took us to this place," Maria Fabiola says. "He made us look at horoscopes in old newspapers. The papers were from the Russian River. And he made us eat canned rabbit food."

"Canned rabbit food?" Shelley Stine says.

"Well, it was canned lettuce," Maria Fabiola says. "Like for rabbits."

Shelly Stine has stopped writing. She turns to me. I'm instantly covered in flop sweat. I can't keep up with whatever Maria Fabiola's doing. "What did the man look like, Eulabee?" she asks.

"Long beard," I say, and then stare at a swirling crack near the ceiling.

"He always wore the same tie-dye shirt and he didn't have any scars," Maria Fabiola adds. "And he had mandalas in the rooms," she says. "And there was a weaving machine."

"A weaving machine?" Shelley Stine asks.

"A loom," I say. I know Maria Fabiola's thinking of the looms we saw when we toured the California missions in third-grade social studies.

"Exactly!" Maria Fabiola says. "You saw it, too."

"Where was this place the man in the tie-dye took you to again?" Shelley Stine asks. She flips her notebook pages back and I struggle to see what else she's written down.

"Near Haight Street," Maria Fabiola says, and again my body sweats all at once. She forges on, leaning toward Shelley Stine. "It was a Victorian house and he took us to the top floor."

"Where near Haight Street?"

"Ashbury," Maria Fabiola says.

"You know there's also a boy that went missing from that area not very long ago," Shelley Stine says, sitting up. "You may have seen his face on milk cartons."

"Oh, he wasn't there," Maria Fabiola says.

"Were there any other girls there?" Shelley Stine asks. "Was Gentle Gordon there?"

"Why would she be there?" I ask.

Shelley Stine turns to me. "She's been missing for a day now."

"But Eulabee, didn't you say you heard someone in the next room, a girl's voice, and the tie-dye guy talking to her?" Maria Fabiola says. She looks at me, and her eyes signal to me *Come on.*

Instead of answering I ask Shelley Stine where Gentle was last seen.

"I'm going to leave it to the detectives to talk to you about that. I don't think I want to say more about Gentle's case right now."

"Okay," Maria Fabiola says. "Wait. Where are the detectives?"

"They're coming by in a bit," Shelley Stine says. "But in the meantime, I want to make sure I understand this correctly. So there was one male kidnapper and he always wore the same tie-dye shirt," Shelley Stine asks. "What color was the shirt?"

"It was red and blue and white tie-dyed together," Maria Fabiola says. "He was very patriotic."

"I see," Shelley Stine says, writing nothing down. The sweat I'm swimming in is now cold. I feel so cold.

I decide I can't talk anymore. Shelley Stine's eyes are giving her away. She knows we're lying. She's having fun now, and I know I'm expelled. Spragg will expel us both and private high schools are out of the question. I picture Ulysses S. Grant High School. I think that's the public I'll be sent to. It's enormous. Thousands of kids and no uniforms. I picture Gentle there, in her bell-bottoms, leaning against a chain-link fence.

"So," Shelley Stine continues. "What do you think was the motive for this kidnapper who always wore the same patriotic blue and red and white tie-dye shirt and served you canned lettuce in a Victorian house and made you read horoscopes from a Russian River newspaper? Why did he want to kidnap you two, do you think?"

"Well, we're like the city's most glamourous flowers, right?" Maria Fabiola says. "We're hothouse flowers."

"Like you need to be kept in a greenhouse?" Shelley Stine says.

"Oh, right," Maria Fabiola says, "you know about this from covering gardening. It's not just that we're kept in greenhouses—that's maybe not what I meant."

"What did you mean then?" Shelley Stine asks. She suddenly looks very tired.

"We're the city's most meaningful flowers," Maria Fabiola says. "We're glamorous and intriguing to the outside world."

"The outside world?" Shelley Stine says. "You mean, like India? France?"

"No," Maria Fabiola says. "Like the rest of San Francisco."

"I see," Shelley Stine says. "Well, I better get going if I'm going to—"

"When's your deadline?" Maria Fabiola asks.

"I'm not sure," Shelley Stine says as she gathers her notebook and pen.

"Well, can I write out what happened to us and give it to you? My thoughts are a jumble," Maria Fabiola says. I look at her and do a double-take: at some point she's started outright crying. "Yesterday Eulabee and I talked and our stories were the same but now I feel so flustered by recounting it all."

Shelley Stine rummages in her bag for tissues and offers them to Maria Fabiola. "That'd be fine," Shelley Stine says. "You can get the story to Mr. Makepeace and he'll get it to me, I'm sure."

Once Shelley Stine's left, Maria Fabiola stands to close the office door. She's no longer crying.

"Well, you were of no help!" she says to me.

"I forgot which story we were going with," I say. "And I just got so confused when she said Gentle was missing."

"That can only help us," Maria Fabiola says. "Three disappearances are better than two, get it?"

"But aren't you worried?" I say.

"About Gentle?" she says. "No. She's a hippie. She's always missing. She *lives* to disappear. I'm worried about *you*. I need to know I can count on you. At this rate, I don't think we're going to make it above the fold. You need to be more supportive when we talk to the detectives. You don't have to tell the story since obviously you're terrible at that, but you can just agree with whatever I say, right? Back me up?"

Mr. Makepeace comes into the office.

"How was it?"

"It was so *painful!*" Maria Fabiola says, and instantly is crying again. "Reliving all those memories was *ghastly!*"

"Here are your tissues," I say, and slide the packet toward her.

30

Ms. Patel escorts us back to our classes and talks the entire way, which is a relief. I need a break from the machinations of Maria Fabiola's mind. I have French class and Maria Fabiola goes to Spanish. In French class Mademoiselle tells us that in Toulouse a restaurant would never serve a salad that required its leaves to be cut with a knife. "Those kinds of salads are for horses," she says. Mademoiselle is young and chic and wears scarves around her neck for the purpose, we suspect, of disguising the many hickeys her boyfriend has given her.

Before class ends, Ms. Patel's face appears at the door. I'm being summoned to the office. The detectives have arrived.

When I get to the office, Maria Fabiola's already there. She stands when she sees me and hugs me as though it's been years. "This time, follow my lead," she says as she pulls me close.

Detective Anderson comes out of the room where she's been speaking with Mr. Makepeace. She's followed by the two male detectives.

"Hello again, Eulabee," Detective Anderson says. "Can you follow me into the office, please?"

Maria Fabiola stands.

"Oh no," Detective Anderson says. "We're going to do one interview at a time. We'll take good care of Eulabee," Detective Anderson assures her.

I follow the detectives to the larger conference room, the same one we were in the first time they interviewed me.

"We're so happy about your safe return home," Detective Anderson says, and holds my eyes for a minute before I turn to look out at the playground. The lower school is having afternoon recess and all the young girls are playing tetherball, four square. The same games we used to play, games with rules.

"We would like to know what happened," Detective Anderson says. "Can you tell us where you've been the last few days?"

I watch a tiny girl send the tetherball round and round until, high on the pole, it runs out of rope and stops.

I know I'm making a choice to not go along with Maria Fabiola's story and I know the consequences—I've experienced them before.

"I wasn't kidnapped," I say. "I was in a shed behind the Olenska School of Ballet on Clement. And then I ran into a cousin and went to his house in West Portal."

"Was Maria Fabiola with you?" Detective Anderson asks.

"Only for a few hours yesterday. She came to the shed to find me because that's where she was when she disappeared."

"Wait. She was in the shed? She wasn't kidnapped?"

"She was hiding in the shed," I say, and I hate myself and know Maria Fabiola will never forgive me. I imagine the years of emotional violence she'll unleash on me and I decide to fight back preemptively.

"Did you coordinate your disappearances beforehand?"

"No," I say. "Hers was based on a book she read."

"On a book she read?"

"Well, a book she skimmed," I say.

The detectives look at each other but don't seem as relieved as I expected. "Thank you Eulabee," Detective Anderson says. "You've saved us a lot of time, and we don't have much. Gentle Gordon is actually missing."

I follow Detective Anderson out to the office's reception area. Maria Fabiola stands and smooths her skirt when she sees us.

"I'm ready," she says to Detective Anderson.

Detective Anderson puts her hand up like she's stopping traffic. "Not now," she says, and she and the other detectives walk out the office door.

That afternoon my mother picks me up from school. She's the first in line so I don't have to wait for the parade of Volvos to make their way up the horseshoe drive. Maria Fabiola sees me get into my mom's car. Her look is baffled.

At home I tell my parents everything. Svea inexplicably prepares a footbath with Epsom salts and places it at the foot of my chair. My mother makes meatballs. My father shows me the letter he received from Christie's, where he brought the Vanessa Bell painting to be appraised. It turns out the painting was a copy. "They think it was someone imitating Bell to teach themselves how to paint," he says.

I go to bed early again. My mother rubs my back with her long nails and I hear my father turning the pages of a book in the next room, the playroom. Ewa is still elsewhere. I can't remember him ever sitting there before. I can see only his knees and the tips of his socks, and watch his feet tapping until I fall away.

I wake up earlier than usual that morning. The clarity of truth is invigorating, I tell myself. I try not to think about the fact that I might be expelled. I go outside in search of the newspaper, to see if any part of Maria Fabiola's story made it into print.

My parents aren't currently subscribing to the *Chronicle* so I have to walk up the street until I find a copy I can read. Almost at the top of El Camino del Mar I find a paper in the bushes. I open it. "SEA CLIFF TEEN STRANGLED—BODY FOUND IN PANHANDLE." I collapse on the sidewalk and scan the article out of order. "Police have no leads . . ." "The death of Gentle Gordon . . ." "Troubled young woman abandoned by her mother . . ." "Struggled with substance abuse . . ." "Body showed signs of struggle . . ." "Found next to the seesaw . . ."

I sit up and read it from start to finish, all the while not believing that it's not me and not Maria Fabiola. Then I have a terrible thought: *Of course it was Gentle. The rest of us were never at risk. Of course it was Gentle.* The words become a mantra I can't end.

My legs begin running downhill. I run past the house where Jefferson Starship used to live and where China's long swing used to hang above the ocean, but the swing is gone and so is Starship. I run past the house that used to give out King Size Hershey's candy bars every Halloween, and past the house that belonged to Carter the Great and is now rented out by the president of a bank. I run past the house where a classmate's hair caught on fire when she was blowing out her birthday candles. I run past the house with the turret, the house where, briefly, I took in the newspapers. I race past the house where the mom uses a wheelchair—we never learned why. I see my own house on the right, looking so compact between the immense houses that border it. I turn away and keep running.

I run past palm trees and I run past gardeners with their trucks and loud leaf blowers and grating rakes. My body is sweating and cooled by the fog as I approach China Beach. My feet make a galloping sound as they race down the ninety-three steps. The beach is empty this gloomy morning. Once on the sand, I hastily remove my shoes and socks. I run to the water's edge and the cold ocean licks my toes. Without touching my face I can feel that it's wet with fog and tears and sweat. I stand there, on the cusp of the ocean and listen to its loud inhale. And then it recedes and takes everything from my childhood with it—the porcelain dolls, the tap-dancing shoes, the concert ticket stubs, the tiny trophies, and the long, long swing.

2019

We are almost fifty years old and the streets of Sea Cliff are no longer ours. The houses that follow the curve of the bay belong to the new San Francisco, to the tech giants, to buyers from abroad who, rumor has it, paid cash and bought the houses sight unseen. The "For Sale" signs were not up for long, and now the driveways remain empty and the curtains stay closed. Our parents' generation laments the new money that's changed the neighborhood, and we and the rest of the world roll our collective eyes.

The venture capitalists have taken over Pacific Heights. The young tech workers have claimed Hayes Valley, Mission Bay, and Potrero Hill—neighborhoods close to the freeway so they have easier commutes to Silicon Valley. But the CEOs and the names behind the companies live in Sea Cliff, where there is privacy and unobstructed views of the Golden Gate. Sea Cliff is for solitude, for when you want to protect yourself from people. Of course, everything is extra fortified now—there are more gates, more cameras.

But the kitchens are too small. The Silicon Valley pioneers want bigger kitchens, bigger closets and windows, higher ceilings, and their new homes in Sea Cliff are always under construction and never finished. They are encased in white plastic, roof to foundation—to hide the location of their tunnels and panic rooms?—while the drilling and hammering drown out the foghorns and crashing waves and every sound of our childhood.

The houses of Sea Cliff no longer belong to our parents—they have passed away or downsized to smaller homes. We don't live in Sea Cliff either. None of us who grew up there, or in almost any other neighborhood in San Francisco, can afford to live where we were raised—not that we necessarily want to. Symphonies of tiny violins play themselves to shreds.

The disappearances of Sea Cliff girls in the eighties is still part of the lore. The newspapers called what happened the Sea Cliff Seizures, and the name stuck. Before the internet I was able to remain fairly anonymous and, upon meeting me, few knew I had been one of the three missing girls. After being expelled from Spragg, I went to Grant High, Gentle's school. Sometimes I imagined I saw her in the hallways and I'd follow her until a head turned and I realized it wasn't her—of course it wasn't. At Grant I sought out friends who were studious and steady and my four years passed unremarkably. At UC Santa Cruz I found the work of Fernando Pessoa and took up Portuguese. Another excuse not to learn Swedish, my mother said. She was probably right.

I married early (he was a fellow undergrad, from San Diego) and we realized our mistake on our honeymoon. We had spent months planning our modest wedding at a sheltered cove north of San Francisco. But after our friends and family departed, we quickly learned we had little to say to each other. We ate meal after meal at the same unsteady table in the same small wooden lodge overlooking the Pacific. In the span of a few days we'd become one of those couples who sit across from each other and eat in silence. We quickly grew tired of listening to each other chew.

I felt ashamed when we divorced, just as I had felt shame about everything that happened in my final year at Spragg—my alleged disappearance, my expulsion. I had made multiple mistakes, witnessed by many. The geography of California was so embedded in my past, in my missteps, that I decided I had to flee.

I was twenty-five when I arrived in Lisbon and was struck by the extent to which it twinned San Francisco: both cities were built on seven hills, both were proud of their red bridges and cable cars, both had suffered the surprise of earthquakes, and were perched on the precipices of continents. I began working as a translator. It wasn't a growth market, but it was steady enough work. I translated hotel brochures, menus for restaurants, terrifying religious pamphlets.

In my thirties, I began translating short novels by a Portuguese writer named Inês Batista whose talents were being discovered later in life. Inês's books were deeply personal meditations on resilience and her working-class upbringing. They were also very funny, as was she. We met more often than most writers meet with their translators—her fortitude reminded me of my mother, who had passed quickly, quietly, a few years after my divorce. As for Inês, she said I was the daughter-in-law she wished she had.

One day, she brought her grown and newly single son, Lucas, to our meeting at a café in the Alfama district. Lucas was handsome and humble, with a faint lisp. He was wearing dark indigo jeans, and as we talked I began to notice that his face, especially the area around his mouth, was taking on a bluish hue. Soon his chin looked like it had grown a blue beard. It was the pants, I realized—they were new and hadn't yet been washed. His hands were on his lap and then on his face as we ate, transferring the color. Inês and I pointed this out to him and he excused himself to use the restroom to wash up.

I didn't know what I found more endearing—the fact that he had purchased new pants because, as I learned, his mother had specifically suggested he not wear his usual athletic attire to meet me. Or that when he returned to the table, no longer blue, he was laughing at himself. It was particularly funny, he said, because it had happened before.

A year after that initial meeting, Lucas and I married. At the age of forty-four I returned to San Francisco to live, bringing with me Lucas, and our son, Gabriel, who was a newborn. We found a small but comfortable place on the north side of North Beach, near to my father's new home. He'd sold the house in Sea Cliff to a family with two ginger-haired boys, who, when I occasionally drive through the neighborhood, I see playing lacrosse on the street. I often send updates about Sea Cliff to Svea, who moved to Uppsala, near Stockholm. She lives close to Linnaeus' Garden, with her partner, a quiet and considerate Swede.

When I returned to San Francisco, I contacted Faith, who was now a pediatrician. Gabriel was born with an arrhythmia, and I brought him to her office for check-ups. She was attentive to Gabriel as she monitored his rapid heartbeat, and she was reassuring to me and Lucas. One day Faith suggested a walk along Land's End, just the two of us. On our walk along the high cliffs she told me about her wife and her two daughters, who she sent to Spragg. She said it had been a great school for girls with two moms.

"As you can imagine, it's changed a lot," she said and stopped walking. "I still can't believe you got kicked out and Maria Fabiola didn't. Her parents must have paid someone off, don't you think?"

"You're more upset about it than I am," I said, looking at her flushed neck. "I think I got used to the glitter Maria Fabiola put on everything." What I didn't admit to Faith then was sometimes I missed the glitter, too.

I occasionally saw Julia, who never spoke of Gentle, but whose secure and safe life seemed to be orchestrated in reaction to her death. She was married to a private equity banker and lived in a house in Tiburon that had once been a school. She dressed in clothes that were usually worn by older women of a certain class and era—Ferragamo shoes with low heels and tidy bows, Ann Taylor turtlenecks. She always carried an umbrella if the forecast hinted at rain.

Through Faith and Julia I was reunited with many former classmates from Spragg, even those I hadn't known well. We sometimes met at the Big 4 Restaurant at the Huntington Hotel where we sat for hours in green leather chairs in front of old posters for the Central Pacific railroad. It was there that we exchanged stories of sadness and small triumphs. We laughed more now than we had as girls, and we found humor in how little we had known.

Almost everyone had returned to San Francisco, it seemed, except for Maria Fabiola. No one knew what had become of her after she'd left for St. George's, a boarding school in Rhode Island. Her family had moved to the East Coast around the same time. No one could track her down on social media—she had most likely married or changed her name. There were rumors she'd moved to Paris and her husband was a designer. There were rumors she'd moved to Uruguay and started a restaurant on the beach. We were approaching fifty and the speculation that swirled around her had not ceased.

It's my work as a translator that ultimately leads me to see Maria Fabiola again. My mother-in-law, Inês, is invited to speak at a literary festival on the island of Capri. Her publisher contacts me, asking if I'll translate for the English-speaking portion of the audience. Inês is approaching eighty, a widow, and doesn't like to travel alone.

When her publisher forwards the details of Inês's event, they include a link to the hotel where the festival's participants will be staying. I spend half an hour admiring the photos. I've never been to Capri—I've never stayed in such luxurious accommodations. We meet in Naples and spend a night in a hotel with a view of Vesuvius. Inês's gray hair is longer than when I last saw her a year ago, her eyes glassy. Her body is slightly more frail but she still has the same distinctive walk: she lifts her knees high and places each foot firmly on the ground, as though snowshoeing. She and I sit side by side on the Naples rooftop. She's working on a new novel, she tells me, about an older woman who falls in love with a young man. *"Você vai traduzir esse livro?"* she asks. I tell her of course I'll translate it. Every book, I assume, will be her last, but sometimes I think she'll live forever. She has not given up, has ceded nothing.

We take a ferry to Capri the next morning. In an hour we're there, under the white cliffs draped in green. We're driven up a steep hill in a golf cart, and then must travel by foot to Anacapri, where cars are not allowed. We walk along a breezy promenade with its explosion of pink bougainvillea. Birdsong is everywhere but we see no birds. We pass a tasteful advertisement for Inês's festival appearance that evening. I take a photo of her posing in front of it and send it to Lucas.

Inês's event is held outdoors, in the plaza in front of the hotel. Chairs have been set up so the audience can have a view of Inês and of the blue, blue sea. I sit off to the side, translating everything into English for those in the audience wearing headsets. While I'm proud of Inês, my translation job is mediocre. I'm accustomed to having time to pore over the words she writes before choosing the right one in English. But tonight, I need to translate quickly, and worry I'm not doing the poetry of her speech justice. No one seems to notice.

She signs books (she always signs them "With all my love, Inês") and then there is a small dinner on the hotel's patio. A buffet has been set up and candles have been lit. I sit at the round table adjacent to hers so her fans can be near her. Seated at my table is a boy around Gabriel's age, and as I watch him eat his pasta and smear tomato sauce around his mouth, I yearn for my son. When the dinner is over, I accompany Inês to her room. The evening air is warm, the orange blossoms fragrant. The hotel has placed a chocolate cake on her desk.

Walking along a garden path to my room, I hear a woman laughing. The sound comes from one of the private patios that accompany the larger suites. I'm reminded of Maria Fabiola and that crazy laugh of hers. I listen closely to see if it will come again, but I only hear the sound of an Italian woman singing into a microphone. She's been paid to entertain poolside, and has an audience of three.

In my room, I place a pillow over my head so I can sleep undisturbed. I wake up late and miss breakfast. Inês knocks on my door at 10 a.m. She's snuck yogurts and fruits in her capacious purse so that I can eat. I ask what she wants to do that day, and she says she has plans to go to San Michele—the former home of a well-known Swedish doctor, with a man who was at dinner the previous night. Apparently he's learning Portuguese and wants to practice with her. "Any young man, you know, is good research for my book," she says and winks. She can't wink with just one eye, so she shuts both her eyes, and for a moment it looks like she's making a wish.

I decide to spend a couple hours sunbathing and swimming, so I walk down to the green lawn adjacent to the pool and search for a vacant chaise longue. As I get settled in, I watch two of the pool boys, both dressed in white shorts and white shirts, adjust an umbrella for an Italian woman in her seventies wearing a sparkling gold swimsuit. She directs them to move the umbrella to the left, then to the right. My swimsuit, a pale pink one-piece that seemed an homage to Fellini when I packed it, now seems not only muted but dated, too.

It's too hot to read. After ten minutes I place my book on the chair and make my way to the pool. As I stand by the railing, dipping my toes in the water, I watch a woman with long hair emerge from the other side. She's wearing a black bikini, and although she is thin, her bosom balloons over her top. A pool boy awaits her as she steps out. He seems only too happy to wrap her in an oversized white towel. As she turns and walks in my direction, I think *Maria Fabiola*. And then I second-guess myself.

She must sense another set of eyes on her because she turns toward me. After registering who I am, there's a short and meaningful lapse before she forces her mouth to smile.

"Hello, Eulabee," she says. She's still fifteen feet away, her face drawn but beautiful.

I rush toward her. I expect we might hug, but she holds my shoulders and kisses me on both cheeks. It's difficult to decipher whether it's the kind of kiss one gives when greeting a friend or leaving them. Her nonchalance unnerves me. It's been over three decades since our last interaction, but her posture implies I've followed her on vacation against her wishes.

"Come to where I'm sitting," she says. "I have an extra chair set up. I'm *waiting* for my husband." The emphasis is either to inform me I'm just invited to pass the time, or that he's perpetually delaying her. I can't tell which.

The tile is hot on my feet and she must notice my discomfort.

"You should get some sandals," she says, like practical shopping advice is the most natural thing for her to be giving me right now.

"Oh, I have some," I explain, stupidly. "They're just somewhere else right now."

We sit on the lounge chairs she's reserved. They are perfectly shaded by a large umbrella, but still the pool boys come over to adjust it.

"Grazie," she says to them, smiling. She's almost fifty and her smile is still a precious reward. I can see this in the boys' faces.

"Grazie," I echo. The boys don't look at me.

"I think this calls for two glasses of prosecco," she says before ordering from the boys in Italian.

"I can't believe we're at the same hotel," I say.

"Well, it *is* the best hotel in Capri," she says, and looks to the sea so far below.

"Where do you live these days?" I ask casually, as though Spragg classmates haven't spent hours speculating what kind of exotic place Maria Fabiola would be calling home. I expect her to say Barcelona or Rome, or a place I've never heard of, someplace where no one would have come across her.

"We live in Lexington," she says, and I practically gasp. "My husband's business is based in Kentucky and we've been there for years. What about you?"

"San Francisco," I say.

"You never left," she says, while looking disapprovingly at my forehead.

"I lived in Lisbon for years—my husband's from there, and my son was born there. But after my mom passed . . . well, it felt like the right time to move closer to my dad."

She says nothing about my mother's death. "What does your husband do in San Francisco?" she asks.

"He coaches soccer at a high school," I say.

"He volunteers?"

"No, he's the coach at a new school in the Presidio."

She asks about the school, and I tell her about it, and about how San Francisco has changed. For a time, the small talk is very small. We could be two people seated next to each other on an airplane, making casual conversation before putting on headphones and ignoring each other for the remainder of the flight.

A different pool boy approaches carrying two glasses of prosecco. He stares at Maria Fabiola's figure.

"Chin chin," she says, and clinks her glass against mine.

"Chin chin," I say.

She takes half the glass in one sip. "Do you see anyone from Spragg?"

"I do, actually."

"Really? Tell me all the gossip."

And so I tell her about Julia and her house in Tiburon and her practical shoes and turtleneck sweaters. I tell her about Faith and how her children go to Spragg—how much she loves the school.

Maria Fabiola seems strangely uncurious about Faith and Julia. Instead she surprises me by asking about Milla, a girl on the periphery of our friend group, who now owns a gallery. "That's a crazy story," I say.

"Tell me," Maria Fabiola says, and she relaxes into her chair. For a moment I am taken out of time and place—I could be a schoolgirl on China Beach, gossiping with my best friend.

"Milla has this woman she brings with her every-where."

"What do you mean?" Maria Fabiola asks.

"This woman is a kind of advisor," I explain. "She calls her her Intuition."

"Excuse me?"

"Milla doesn't trust her intuition anymore," I say, "so she pays a woman to be her intuition. She brings her everywhere, and consults with her before making any significant decision."

"That's hilarious," she says. "No one wants to do anything for themselves anymore. We've always out-sourced our cooking, our cleaning, our childcare . . ."

I smile. I can't afford to outsource any of these things.

"And now," Maria Fabiola says, "we outsource our intuition!"

She laughs her genuine cascading laugh. "I'm so happy we ran into each other," she says, and for a moment, she does seem very happy. And I feel as I did when I was thirteen—that her laughter is a reward, that her attention is a prize.

A man in pink salmon shorts and a white collared shirt makes his way over to us. As he gets closer it dawns on me that this must be Maria Fabiola's husband. He's older than we are, probably around fifty-five, but still in good physical shape. He looks like a retired tennis pro, his hair just long enough to imply an artistic side.

"Hi honey," she says. "How was tennis?"

I thrill at my guess.

He bends down and kisses her on the cheek. His nose is sunburnt and he smells of sunscreen mixed with sweat.

"I beat him again," he says. Then he looks at me, as though suddenly aware of my presence.

"Eulabee, this is Hugh," Maria Fabiola says. "Hugh, this is a surprise from the past—this is Eulabee."

We shake hands. His fingers are tan, his nails buffed.

"How do you two know each other?" he asks, and for a moment I'm speechless. My husband knew Maria Fabiola's name by our third date.

"We grew up very near each other," Maria Fabiola says.

This is what it's come to. I am a childhood neighbor, nothing more.

"Ah, the mean streets of Sea Cliff!" he says. "So glad you survived. Not many people get out of there alive."

I smile politely and search his face for irony, for knowledge of the reported kidnappings Maria Fabiola and I endured, for awareness of Gentle's death. His face is blank. He knows nothing.

I look at Maria Fabiola and see only my own reflection in her sunglasses.

He asks if I live in the Bay Area still, and I tell him I do. I tell him I'm a translator. Maria Fabiola removes her glasses and squints at me. "You are?"

"Wow, a dying art form," Hugh says. "How long are you staying in Capri?"

"We leave tomorrow," I say. "I'm here with my mother-in-law. And you?"

"A few more nights," he says. "We come every year for a week, sometimes two."

"How lovely," I say, not sounding at all like myself.

"What do you want to do for lunch, babe?" Hugh says to Maria Fabiola. "Should I order you your usual?"

"I'm so tired of eating here," she says and sighs. She turns to me. "I've had the same salad for four days."

"Want to walk to the piazza with me and get a bite?" I suggest.

"I could use a walk," she says. "Do you mind, Hugh?"

He says he doesn't, but I watch him stare at Maria Fabiola as she stands. It takes me a minute to place what I see on his face. It's a look of concern a parent might give a child who's about to take a test for which they are not prepared.

Maria Fabiola pulls on a bright blue dress and slips on crisp white espadrilles. I return to my lounge chair and slide into my flip-flops and a white cover-up that's a few years old and, in the sunlight, appears a shade of buttermilk.

We walk out of the hotel and onto the promenade. Maria Fabiola suggests we go into a Missoni store. "You'll love their material," she says. The saleswoman smiles at Maria Fabiola. I mention I'm looking for a new cover-up, and she pulls out several options for me to try on. While I'm changing, I hear the saleswoman complimenting the color of Maria Fabiola's attire. "It's the color of the famous Blue Grotto," the saleswoman says.

The flattery works. Maria Fabiola tries on a long shimmering blue and green skirt.

"What do you think?" she says, admiring herself in the mirror.

"It looks incredible," I say honestly. "You look like a mermaid."

She buys it on the spot. I marvel at the ease with which she hands over her credit card. "Are you going to get anything?" Maria Fabiola asks me.

"I'll come back later," I lie.

We continue down the promenade. A breeze from the sea below scatters the heat. We pass two Carabinieri talking to a photographer.

"Do you know it's illegal to be a paparazzi here?" Maria Fabiola says. "Yesterday Hugh and I were out on the water and all these fishing boats around us were filled with men with cameras with long lenses. They were desperate to get photos of the party on some rapper's yacht."

I don't know what the correct response is. "Shameful," I say.

We pass a church where a wedding is about to take place. The bridesmaids pose outside with white bouquets. Their dresses are silk, dark fuchsia, and too heavy for this heat.

Maria Fabiola and I approach the piazza. We pick a casual, relatively empty restaurant and sit at a shaded outdoor table. The waiter approaches and we each order a glass of wine and a prosciutto and melon appetizer and caprese salad to share. A boy kicks a soccer ball into the middle of the piazza and I watch as he runs after it.

"Do you have children?" she asks.

"One," I say, "a boy." And then, for no reason, I feel the need to explain. "I became a mom late," I say. "I was married before and it ended. Then I miscarried twice—both times were devastating. I'm happy to have the one." I tell her about Gabriel and how we spend every weekend, it seems, on a train. "He's at that age," I say. I reach for my phone so I can show her a photo.

"Oh, no, let's not be cliché," she says. "Let's try to be European and not bring our phones out on the table."

"Okay," I say, replacing my phone in my bag. I remember how she had a way of making me feel crass. "What about you? Do you have children?"

She hesitates. She stares at me and a smile overtakes her face. "Three daughters," she says.

"Ah, that's like out of a fairy tale," I say.

Her smile vanishes. "What do you mean?" she asks.

"You know, the number three is always in fairy tales. Three bears, three pigs, three daughters. Three's the charm."

"You were always so into reading your stories," she says.

And you were so into making up yours, I want to say. But we've grown up now, and so I refrain.

We drink our wine, we laugh.

Before long, a large table near ours is populated by a group of beautiful young women.

"They must be models," I whisper to Maria Fabiola. She says "Yes" without looking at them. The tables around the models fill quickly. People the world over believe beauty is contagious.

We listen to the models speak accented English with one another. Russian, Slovakian, Dutch, we guess. Three of the four are smoking. Passersby stop, stare, move on. Soon, though, the attention seems to be waning, so one of the models stands up and takes two loping steps into the piazza. "Hey bitches," she says, far too loudly, "can you tell I've been working out?"

All the young women compliment her physique. Now the attention of the piazza, two hundred pairs of eyes, is back upon the table of models. The models look away, feigning disgust.

"I hope my girls don't grow up to be models," Maria Fabiola says. But there is something in her voice that implies that this will be difficult to fight—their beauty will pull them inexorably toward modelhood.

The food arrives and over lunch Maria Fabiola tells me about her daughters. Their names are Simone, Cleo, and Mirabella. The youngest is interested in ballet, the two older girls play tennis, like their father.

The church bells start to clang loudly. We watch the newly married couple emerge from the small church, holding hands. Everyone in the restaurant and in the piazza stands and applauds. The bride's and groom's eyes blink quickly, like newborns adjusting to the light.

"So how much time do you spend translating?" she asks, turning toward me.

"A lot," I say. "It's what I do."

"That's really your job?" she says. "Like your profession?"

"It's on my business card," I say and shrug.

"Can I see?" she says.

"My card?" I ask, taken aback. "Sure, I just got new ones." I open my purse and hand one to her.

She studies the card and turns it over. In her hands I see that the paper stock is flimsy. She turns her profile to me as she looks out into the distance. "Sorry I'm so distracted," she says, "but I'm here on business."

I can tell she's waiting for me to ask what kind of business and so I do.

"I'm thinking about buying the hotel."

"The hotel we're staying in?"

"Yes," she says. "And maybe the festival, too."

"It's for sale?" I ask.

"Oh, Eulabee," she says. "Everything is for sale."

I try to catch her eye, but she starts looking through her purse for something. "Ah, found it," she says, and produces a tube of lipstick.

To get back to the hotel we have to return the same way we came. I take in the fact we are together on the promenade with the electric blue water below. We spent much of our youth walking side by side, and here we are again, on another cliff, above another ocean.

"I've been wanting to ask you something," I say and pause.

We continue walking and she looks away, at the many boats below, as though something has caught her attention, as though knowing what I'm going to ask.

"What do you think happened that day when we walked to school and there was the white car . . . ?" I say. I try to speak casually, but it comes out sounding planned.

"What?" she says.

"Remember the white car? There was a man in it, and the police were called and came to school." I look at her to see if she really could have forgotten.

We walk in silence for a minute longer.

"Yeah," she says. "That was really weird."

"Yup," I say.

Yeah, she said. Yup, I said.

I look at her and try to see her eyes through her Celine glasses. But her silence and her body, which is tense, tell me I have lost her again.

When we return to the hotel, she holds my shoulders with her hands and kisses me on both cheeks. This is the exact way she greeted me at the pool.

I dine with Inês and several of the other festival authors and translators. The restaurant is elegant and we are all underdressed. Inês talks about her day at San Michele, and how the owner of the estate, someone named Munthe, was the personal doctor to Queen Victoria of Sweden, who was unhappily married to King Gustaf. Munthe required the queen come to him on Capri for treatment, and everyone suspected that their relationship was more than that of doctor and patient. This story is discussed and laughed about through the first three courses. But after the fourth, we each look at the menu, discreetly trying to ascertain how many courses are left before we can leave.

We excuse ourselves before dessert—we blame jet lag (me) and old age (Inês)—and walk arm-in-arm down the maze of steps that will eventually take us to the hotel. We stop to ask directions from local residents walking their well-groomed dogs. Back at the hotel I escort Inês to her room. She seems worn out by the trip, and disappointed in the day. I think she had romantic intentions for the young man who escorted her to San Michele, and things did not pan out as she wished.

I stand on the tiled balcony off my room, staring out at the terra-cotta roof of another hotel. I was looking forward to this weekend and now I just want to be home with my husband and his suede-colored eyes, and my son and his trains and warm hands. For years I wanted to see Maria Fabiola again and talk about what happened with us. I wanted an ending, or an explanation for why she had started the avalanche of lies all those years ago. Instead I met her husband, who had been told so little about her past.

I see Hugh at breakfast. He's wearing a peach collared shirt and eating alone at a table set with silver. Maria Fabiola is skipping breakfast because she doesn't want to run into me.

"Good morning," I say to him.

"Good morning," he says, and wipes his mouth. He stands and gestures for me to join him at the table. I sit and he helps push my chair in before returning to his seat.

"Heading off today?" he asks.

I tell him my mother-in-law is packing and after breakfast we'll take the ferry back. He gives me a recommendation of a restaurant he loves in Naples and tells me the name of the maître d'. This is what the wealthy do, I think. They spend their expensive meals talking about other expensive meals.

The waiter comes by and offers me a cappuccino. "Signora Batista was already here," he says. "You missed her."

"Yes," I say. "I slept in."

"Hotels," Hugh muses when the waiter has left. "They know everybody's business. They probably know my wife is having a massage right now. She's the only person I know who gets massages at ten in the morning."

Hugh is easy to talk to. I have forgotten what he does for a living and settle into thinking of him as a tennis pro. His conversation is an intermediate lesson given to a new pupil. He lobs me a ball and waits for me to hit it back. If I miss, he serves me another ball.

Hugh tells me he's happy to meet me since he has met so few of his wife's friends from childhood, from San Francisco. "I always imagine what it would be like to live there," he says. "My company has an office near Cupertino so I could make the switch. We know a man who works in real estate. High-end properties. His name is Wallenberg. Do you know him?"

"I used to," I say. The last time I saw Axel Wallenberg in person was at the welcome-back party for Maria Fabiola. "He went to a different school."

"That's right. It must have been so strange for you women to grow up in an all-girls school. You know what Maria always says."

My eyes open wide. He calls her Maria.

"She says that you were all molded into being replicas of one another. She says the only way out was to be extraordinary."

I'm at a loss for words. "Well, she *is* extraordinary," I finally say.

He smiles a polite smile. This is something he hears often. He signals to the waiter that he'd like coffee.

"Do you think if you moved to the Bay Area you'd send your daughters to Spragg?" I ask.

Hugh stares at me. "My daughters?" he says. Something about the way he looks at me makes me fearful. "Who told you I had daughters?" he asks.

Oh god, I think. "Maria Fabiola told me . . ." I say. "She told me about her three daughters."

"Can we go outside for a minute?" he says and stands without waiting for my response.

We walk out onto the balcony and find two middle-aged women admiring each other's bracelets. "No," he mumbles and turns. I follow him to a staircase off the rear of the breakfast room. He suddenly looks like a man who desperately needs a vacation, not like a man who is in the midst of one.

"You have to understand," he says, as though he is going to tell me the secret to life. But instead of sharing he is so silent I can hear the still air. "She does this . . . ," he starts to say.

A maid ascends the staircase with fresh tablecloths. She seems surprised to see us there. "*Scusatemi*," she says, but Hugh seems unaware of his surroundings and barely moves to let her by. She hustles past us.

"We don't have daughters," he says and opens his fists like a magician at the end of a trick. "We'll probably never see you again, but I wanted to correct the record in case you talk to your other friends." Hugh looks at me meaningfully. It's clear he's been in a situation like this before.

I stare out at the ocean. I think back to my lunch with Maria Fabiola. Of course she said she had three children. I had one, and had two miscarriages. That made three. I contemplate asking Hugh if Maria Fabiola's really planning to buy the hotel, the festival, but suddenly I'm exhausted, and besides, I know the answer.

Inês and I take the funicular down to the port, and board our ferry. She wants to sit on top and secures two seats near the bow. "You know that Homer wrote about this island," she says.

I ask her to remind me. I haven't read *The Odyssey* since Mr. London's class.

"This is where the sirens called from, where they lured the sailors to their deaths. Odysseus put wax in the ears of his sailors so they wouldn't hear their song.

But Odysseus wanted to hear it, so he tied himself to the mast so he could listen without being tempted."

The ferry pulls away from the port.

"I'm thirsty," Inês says. "Are you?"

I walk downstairs to the snack bar. As I'm returning, my phone begins to ring. The call is from a number I don't recognize, so I ignore it.

A second later I get a text. It's a photo of three beautiful, dark-haired girls. Another text comes through. "My babies," it says.

Maria Fabiola has my number from my business card. I zoom in on the photo. I'm not sure whose three girls they are, but she did a good job—they look like her, ethereal-eyed and with her full lips.

Inês is watching Naples coming toward us at a turtle's pace. I hand her a bottle of water and sit next to her, inhaling her nutmeg scent.

Another text comes through. Maria Fabiola is asking me to submit the photo of the girls to the Spragg alumnae bulletin. "Simone is the troublemaker," one says. "Cleo is the peacemaker," says another. "Mirabella is the enigma," says another. "A little bit like you."

The texts keep coming, the arrival of each announced by the phone's loud sing-song alert. "Hope they don't turn out like those models yesterday!" reads one, followed by "Bitches!"

"That was a joke because of the models!" reads the next.

I turn down the volume and place the phone deep in my bag.

When we arrive in Naples, the ferry lurches forward, and then back before righting itself. The passengers all rush to the doors. I gather our suitcases and help Inês off the boat. My phone rings again, louder now. The jostling in the bag must have turned the volume back up.

I look behind me at Capri, as though I can see Maria Fabiola there calling, calling.

"Who keeps trying to reach you?" Inês asks.

"Long story," I say.

We're surrounded by tourists rushing to get onto the ferry, to go where we've been. I steer our suitcases through the throng. I'm sweating in the heat.

"This way," I say, leading us in the opposite direction of the bright blue sea, but the ringing only grows louder.

Acknowledgments

What would I do without my family? Thank you to my parents, Paul and Inger, and to my sister, Vanessa, for so much, for everything, for a lifetime of kindness. Thank you to Dave for endless encouragement and countless reads, and to our kids, for constant inspiration and for this book's title.

Enormous thanks to my incomparable agent, Nicole Aragi, and to Edwidge Danticat for introducing us. Thank you to everyone at Aragi Inc. and to Brooke Ehrlich at Anonymous Content. I'm indebted to my longtime editor, Daniel Halpern, and to Gabriella Doob for all her work on behalf of this novel. Thank you also to Helen Atsma, Sonya Cheuse, Elizabeth Yaffe, Michelle Crowe, Lydia Weaver, Leda Scheintaub, and everyone at Ecco. Thank you also to my foreign advocates and publishers: Felicity Rubinstein at Lutyens &

Rubinstein, Karen Duffy and everyone at Atlantic, and Lina Muzur at Hanser.

I'm so grateful to my fellow McSweeney's board members, especially those whose support during the writing of this book nurtured me in innumerable ways: to Gina Pell for many conversations about literature in general and this novel in particular, to both Isabel Duffy and Caterina Fake for literally giving me the keys to quiet spaces in which to work when I was nearing the finish line, and to Natasha Boas for her advice about covers. Enormous thanks as well to Amanda Uhle, Hilary Kivitz, and Brian Dice, and to Bibiana Liete for help with my Portuguese translation questions.

I'm also grateful to Jennifer Bunshoft and Nínive Calegari for answering my questions, and to Eve Weinsheimer for her great eye, and to Em-J Staples for her close read. Charlotte Trounce: thank you for the stunning cover art.

And thank you to my writer friends, those indulgers and truthsayers, who read so many drafts of this book: Ann Packer, Rafael Yglesias, Sarah Stone, Ron Nyren, Lisa Michaels, Angela Pneuman, Ann Cummins, Steven Willis, Cornelia Nixon, Tiffany Shlain, Rachel Lehmann-Haupt, and Amanda Eyre Ward. My deepest thanks to Heidi Julavits for her wise edits and decades of friendship.

About the Author

VENDELA VIDA is the award-winning author of six books, including *Let the Northern Lights Erase Your Name* and *The Diver's Clothes Lie Empty*. She is a founding editor of *The Believer* magazine, and co-editor of *The Believer Book of Writers Talking to Writers* and *Confidence, or the Appearance of Confidence*, a collection of interviews with musicians. She was a founding board member of 826 Valencia, the San Francisco writing center for youth, and lives in the Bay Area with her family.